THE BEAST OF BASKERVILLE

STARSCAPE BOOKS BY ANNETTE CASCONE AND GINA CASCONE

DEADTIME STORIES®

Grave Secrets

The Witching Game

The Beast of Baskerville

Invasion of the Appleheads (coming soon)

DEADTIME STORIES

THE BEAST OF BASKERVILLE

ANNETTE CASCONE and GINA CASCONE

STARSCAPE

A TOM DOHERTY ASSOCIATES BOOK · NEW YORK

THE BEAST OF BASKERVILLE

Copyright © 2012 by Annette Cascone and Gina Cascone

Invasion of the Appleheads excerpt © 2012 by Annette Cascone and Gina Cascone

Deadtime Stories® is a registered trademark of Annette Cascone and Gina Cascone.

Deadtime Stories logo by Bill Villareal

A Starscape Book
Published by Tom Doherty Associates, LLC
175 Fifth Avenue
New York, NY 10010

www.tor-forge.com

ISBN 978-0-7653-3067-3

First Edition: May 2012

Printed in the United States of America

0 9 8 7 6 5 4 3 2 1

For our old gang of friends from Academy Manor, thanks for the memories—and for making growing up so much fun.

THE BEAST OF BASKERVILLE

1

Adam Riley started to sweat as he and his best friend, Eugene Nazzaro, slowly approached the long gravel drive that snaked its way up to the creepy old house on the hill. It was the Leeds house, where the Beast of Baskerville had been born, the house where the sniveling, snorting, subhuman creature lived now.

From the street, Adam could see all the warning signs telling him to turn tail and run. They were nailed to the rotted-out trees that lined the drive:

KEEP OUT! PRIVATE PROPERTY!

NO TRESPASSING ALLOWED!

ENTER AT YOUR OWN RISK!

Adam swallowed hard. The last thing in the world he wanted to do was climb Deadman's Hill.

But the creature was expecting him.

Here goes nothing, Adam thought, taking a deep breath to steady his nerves. He lifted his foot and crossed over the imaginary safety line between Ridge Road and the Leedses' driveway.

Behind him, Eugene stopped dead in his tracks.

"This is not a good idea," Eugene told Adam for the twelve millionth time. "You're only asking for trouble."

"But if I don't deal with this now, I'm dead tonight!" Adam exclaimed.

"And what are you going to do when the little beast throws a big fat tizzy fit?" Eugene asked. "That's what will happen, you know—the minute you tell him you're not coming to his stupid birthday party tonight."

Adam knew Eugene was right.

J.J. Leeds, the thirteen-year-old, sniveling, snorting, subhuman creature that had moved into the Beast of Baskerville's old house, was definitely going to throw a major tizzy fit. Especially when he found out that *no one* in the neighborhood was planning to come to his party.

"You're not going to tell J.J. about anyone else, are you?" Eugene wanted to know.

"Are you nuts?" Adam shot back. "Then I'll really be dead. Because everyone in the neighborhood will kill me!"

Adam didn't even want to tell J.J. that he wasn't coming to the party, but thanks to his mom, he didn't have a choice.

Mrs. Riley felt sorry for J.J. Leeds. She insisted that the only reason all the neighborhood kids picked on him was because his last name was Leeds, just like the Beast's.

Adam had tried to explain to his mother that the problem with J.J. wasn't his name at all. Lots of people in Baskerville were named Leeds, including Stacey Leeds, one of Adam's good friends. The Leeds family had founded the town of Baskerville more than two hundred years ago, and dozens of Leedses were still scattered about.

It wasn't even the fact that J.J. and his mom had

moved into the creepiest house in town that made him a spitball target. If J.J. had been a normal kid, everyone in the neighborhood, except for Eugene, probably would have thought that was cool.

But J.J. wasn't a normal kid. He was a sniveling, snorting, loogie-spitting little beast. And everyone in the neighborhood knew it. Everyone but Mrs. Riley.

"I can't believe your mom is making you do this," Eugene said.

"Me neither," Adam groaned. "But if I don't tell J.J. face-to-face that I'm not coming to his party later, my mom won't let me sleep out tonight. And if I don't give him this stupid present, she'll make me go to his party."

"So why don't you just leave the present in the mailbox and tell your mom he wasn't home?" Eugene suggested.

Adam considered that idea for a second. But he knew it wouldn't work. "I can't," he told Eugene. "My mom might call Mrs. Leeds. Then I'll really be in trouble."

J.J.'s mom was always at home. She didn't own a car, and she rarely went out.

J.J. claimed that Mrs. Leeds had to stay inside because she was allergic to the air on the outside.

No one believed it. Mrs. Leeds was just creepy, and she was another reason no one wanted to go to J.J.'s party.

"So what do you want to do?" Eugene asked, cringing. "Talk to Mrs. Leeds?"

Adam shot him a look. "No, I don't want to talk to Mrs. Leeds! But if my mom does, she'll know I didn't even ring the doorbell."

None of the kids in the neighborhood had ever even seen Mrs. Leeds since she and J.J. moved in, except through the windows of her house. She was usually up in the "Beast Tower," sitting in front of the stained-glass window, rocking back and forth in her chair, watching to make sure no one stepped foot on her property.

It was Mrs. Leeds who'd put up all the warning signs to keep the neighborhood kids out.

"Oh, man," Eugene sighed. "This is a nightmare."

"Tell me about it," Adam agreed.

"Why's your mother being such a bedbug about this anyway?" Eugene wondered.

"Because she feels bad that J.J. doesn't have any friends in the neighborhood," Adam explained. "And she doesn't want me to be mean."

"Yeah, well, J.J. doesn't have any friends *outside* the neighborhood, either," Eugene pointed out.

"I know," Adam said. "But my mom thinks that's because Mrs. Leeds didn't send him to school, not because he's a booger ball."

"Mrs. Leeds didn't *have* to send him to school, remember?" Eugene mocked. "J.J.'s a genius."

"Yeah, right." Adam smirked. "J.J.'s a real genius. He doesn't even know his first name."

He didn't, either. J.J. insisted that the *J*s were his name, not just initials.

"No way that kid has a three thousand I.Q.," Eugene said, shaking his head.

"No kidding," Adam said. "I.Q.s don't even go up that high, you moron. He made that up."

But J.J. had sworn it was true. He claimed he was so smart, he didn't have to go to school.

"Let's just get this over with," Adam said impatiently, taking a step up the drive.

"Sorry, pal." Eugene's feet were still planted on the safe side of the imaginary line. "From here on in, you're on your own. No way I'm climbing Deadman's Hill."

"It's just a driveway," Adam huffed.

"Oh, yeah?" Eugene shot back. "Tell that to the Beast of Baskerville's victims."

"That's just a stupid legend," Adam told him.

"Then how come everyone knows this is the Beast's house?" Eugene demanded.

"*Was* his house," Adam corrected, "more than two hundred years ago. And no one knows that for sure."

"*Everyone* knows that for sure," Eugene protested. "And everyone knows this is the hill he dragged all his victims up—right before he tore them to shreds and buried them in his well."

"What well?" Adam asked. "Do you see a well on this property?"

"Nooooo," Eugene replied. "But that doesn't mean it's not here."

Adam stared at Eugene. Apparently, J.J. wasn't the only genius in the neighborhood. "If you can't *see* the well, then how can it be here?"

"Maybe it's hidden," Eugene suggested.

Adam rolled his eyes. "How the heck do you hide a three-thousand-pound tunnel made out of stone?"

"Who knows," Eugene answered. "When witches are involved, anything is possible."

"What witches?" Adam asked, exasperated.

"The witches that cursed Elvira," Eugene told him. "The ones that turned Jimmy Leeds into the Beast before he was born."

Elvira Leeds was supposedly the Beast of Baskerville's mother. She was also a witch. According to legend, Elvira Leeds married a mortal back in the 1700s when the town of Baskerville was first founded. And because she broke the rules of her coven, which stated that witches could marry only warlocks, the other witches cursed her. They turned her husband into a three-headed newt with one eye. Then they put a spell on her unborn child.

When Elvira Leeds finally gave birth to her son, Jimmy, he was only half human. His arms and legs were normal, but the rest of him was beastly.

Two twisted horns shot out of his skull, while two

goatlike hooves grew in place of ten human toes. His eyes burned red like flames. And every inch of his body was covered with matted black hair.

Jimmy Leeds was supposedly so hideous that his witchy mother tossed him down the well on her property, hoping to be rid of him.

But Jimmy Leeds didn't die. Instead, he grew into the Beast. Rumor had it that every so often, Jimmy Leeds had climbed out of the well to feed on innocent children.

Some people, like Eugene, believed he still did.

"You know what?" Adam sighed in frustration. "You're a yo-yo. There is no well. And there's no Beast of Baskerville, either. Now are you coming with me or what? Because if you don't come with me, I'll tell J.J. about tent night tonight," he threatened.

"You wouldn't dare!" Eugene turned pale.

"Would too," Adam lied. "And I'll tell everyone that *you're* the one who told him."

"Tent night" was another reason no one wanted to go to J.J.'s party. All the kids in the neighborhood had been planning to sleep out for weeks. They were all setting up tents in their backyards. Then, when the parents were in bed for the night, the kids were going to sneak out of their yards to play kick the can and hang out.

Needless to say, J.J. wasn't invited.

"I mean it," Adam bluffed. "And I'll tell J.J. you want him to sleep in our tent."

Eugene gave in. "I'll go with you, okay?" he agreed in a panic. "But if something bad happens to us on this hill, I'm blaming you."

"Nothing bad is going to happen to us," Adam assured him.

But Adam was wrong.

Something bad *was* going to happen to them—but not on the hill.

2

I ought to have my head examined for this," Eugene complained. He plunked himself down in the street and started to untie his sneakers.

"What the heck are you doing?" Adam asked.

"I'm taking off my sneakers," Eugene told him.

"Why?"

"Because there's no way I'm climbing Deadman's Hill in these shoes," Eugene explained. "My scent is all over them."

"Your what?" Adam was sure he'd heard wrong.

But Adam's ears weren't the problem. The problem was the loose screw rattling around Eugene's head.

"My scent!" Eugene repeated, as if Adam were daft. "It's all over these sneakers."

"What are you talking about?" Adam groaned.

"Protecting myself," Eugene told him, "from the Beast."

"Let me get this straight," Adam said. "You're taking your sneakers off to protect yourself from the Beast?"

Eugene nodded.

"And how is that supposed to work?" Adam wanted to know.

"If I take my sneakers off, the Beast won't be able to smell me," Eugene answered.

"Are you nuts?" Adam exclaimed. "Everyone in the neighborhood will be able to smell you!"

"Very funny," Eugene shot back. "But if I don't wear my shoes up Deadman's Hill, the Beast can't hunt me down."

"Who told you that?" Adam asked.

"Dougie," Eugene said.

Adam rolled his eyes. Dougie Dembrowski was one of their neighborhood friends. His hobby was to torture Eugene with scary Beast of Baskerville stories.

The stories were always made up. But Eugene was afraid of his own shadow, so Dougie could always get one over on him.

"And how exactly does the Beast hunt you down?" Adam was dying to hear the answer to this one.

"Dougie says that the Beast's sense of smell is so keen, he can pick up B.O. just from the soles of your shoes. Once he has your smell, he knows who you are. Then he can hunt you down anywhere, even in your own backyard. So if I don't wear my shoes, the Beast won't be able to find me."

"Dougie's out of his mind," Adam said.

"He is not," Eugene replied. "Dougie's father's great-great-great-grandfather got eaten by the Beast. All because he climbed Deadman's Hill in his sneakers!"

"Cut me a break." Adam cracked up. "Nobody even had sneakers when Mr. Dembrowski's triple-great-grandfather was alive. Dougie's just messing with you again."

"How do you know?" Eugene asked defensively. "Maybe they were old people's sneakers or something."

"First of all," Adam said, "Dougie's relatives didn't

even live in Baskerville. They lived in Poland. And secondly, look it up online. There were no sneakers back in the eighteen hundreds!"

"Well, maybe they were shoes," Eugene snapped. "All I know is that I'm taking mine off. No way I'm leaving a trail."

"So what are you going to do? Walk up this gravel in your bare feet so that the Beast can smell your toes?"

"No," Eugene answered. "You are."

"Oh, no, I'm not," Adam told him. "No way I'm walking on these stones without shoes."

"You are if you don't want *me* to tell J.J. about tent night," Eugene threatened.

"Let me ask you a question," Adam said. "If the Beast really was sniffing around Deadman's Hill, why hasn't he eaten J.J. yet? I mean, J.J.'s like the stinkiest person on earth. And he walks up and down this driveway about three thousand times a day."

Eugene was stumped, but he was still getting shoeless.

"You know what?" Adam untied his own laces. "Take my sneakers, you jerk. But when we go up there, I'm telling J.J. that you're not coming to his party, either."

"Fine," Eugene huffed. "But you better tell him that present is from both of us then."

"Fine," Adam huffed back. He threw his sneakers at Eugene and started up the drive in his socks.

"Hey!" Eugene shouted as he tried to bury his "scent" in Adam's shoes. "Wait up! I'm not climbing Deadman's Hill alone!"

But Eugene wasn't going to get the chance to climb Deadman's Hill at all. Just as he stepped over the safety line, a horrible creature grabbed him from behind.

And it wasn't the *little* beast.

3

"A*aaaaaaaagggghhhh!*" Eugene's screams echoed up the hill.

Adam turned to look and froze dead in his tracks. There really were witches in Baskerville! And one of them had Eugene by the back of his collar!

Adam blinked hard, but the bony, hunched woman in the black flowing dress and veil wasn't going away.

This can't be real! Adam cried silently as Eugene wailed like a siren.

"*Let go of me!*" he screamed.

"I'll let go of you all right," the witchy woman croaked

like a frog. "As soon as you tell me what you think you're doing on my property!"

"Nothing!" Eugene protested. "We were just coming to see J.J. Leeds."

"Who's 'we'?" the woman asked, spinning around quickly, her creepy dress billowing around her.

Adam ducked behind one of the rotted-out trees on the drive. But Eugene wasn't about to face his horrible fate all alone.

"Me and Adam," Eugene revealed as he pointed up the drive.

"You!" the woman bellowed, zeroing in on Adam's tree. "Get over here right now!"

Adam's knees were knocking together so hard as he stepped into view, they were already turning black and blue.

"What do you want with my J.J.?" the woman croaked again.

"*Your* J.J.?" Adam gulped.

"Yes," she snapped. "*My* J.J. I am his mother, after all."

Holy smokes! Adam thought. *This isn't a witch. This is Mrs. Leeds!*

Adam couldn't believe his eyes. Seeing Mrs. Leeds out of the house was even more startling than seeing a witch.

"So what do you want with my J.J.?" Mrs. Leeds demanded again. "He's not home. In fact, I'm looking for him now. You haven't seen him, have you?"

Eugene shook his head hard enough to pull free from Mrs. Leeds's grip.

"No," Adam answered, shaking his head, too. "We haven't seen him. We only came over to tell him that we won't be able to make it to his birthday party tonight."

"What birthday party?" she growled.

Adam and Eugene exchanged looks.

"This birthday party," Adam said, pulling J.J.'s goofy elephant invitation from the pocket of his shorts.

Mrs. Leeds grabbed it from his hand. "Well, well, well," she cackled. "The little genius thinks he's going to put one over on me, does he?"

Adam had no idea what Mrs. Leeds was talking about. And he didn't want to know, either—especially when Mrs. Leeds ripped the elephant's head off and tore the invitation to shreds.

"Looks like my little J.J. is in for another rude awakening," she mumbled, more to herself than to them.

Eugene whispered in Adam's ear. "Just give her the present and let's get out of here," he said.

"Good idea," Adam whispered back. Then he cleared his throat and held out the box. "Anyway," he told Mrs. Leeds, "would you just tell J.J. that we're sorry we can't come to his party tonight, and give him this present."

Eugene elbowed Adam hard in the ribs.

"It's from both of us," Adam added. "Adam and Eugene," he clarified.

"Keep your stupid present," Mrs. Leeds snarled at them viciously. "There's not going to be a birthday party for J.J.! Not ever!" She tossed the purple elephant pieces into the air. "Now get off my driveway," she shouted, "before I call the police and tell them I've got Beast of Baskerville trespassers again!"

Adam wasn't about to argue with Mrs. Leeds. He tucked the present under his arm and took off behind Eugene.

Unfortunately, Eugene slammed into another Leeds a second later.

"Hey!" J.J. complained as he tried not to drop the huge white cake box he was carrying. "Watch where you're going!"

On top of the cake box was a bag full of purple party hats that toppled to the ground.

"Sorry, J.J.," Eugene apologized as Adam slammed into *him*.

"You could at least help me," J.J. snorted as he shoved the box at Eugene. Then he wiped his snotty nose with the back of his hand and bent down to pick up his party hats.

Behind them, Mrs. Leeds let out a roar. "J.J.!" she hollered from the bottom of Deadman's Hill. "Get your little butt over here right now!"

"Uh-oh!" J.J. yelped, cramming his party hats back into the bag. "What's my mom doing out?"

"I think she's looking for you," Adam said.

"How do you know that?" J.J. asked.

"Because that's what she said," Eugene told him.

"You talked to my mom?" J.J. shrieked. His foul breath floated up Adam's nostrils.

"Yeah," Adam said, choking on the words, "just a few minutes ago."

"You didn't tell her about my party tonight, did you?" J.J. asked in a panic.

Adam and Eugene exchanged guilty looks. But they didn't have to answer, because Mrs. Leeds did.

"What's all this nonsense about a birthday party?" she barked as she stormed over and grabbed J.J. by the ear. "We don't celebrate birthdays in this house. And we don't throw parties, either."

J.J. started to shake.

"Birthday parties are for other people," Mrs. Leeds ranted. She pulled the cake box out of Eugene's hands and tossed it across the street. "Now get in that house and get to your chores!" she shouted.

Adam and Eugene exchanged horrified looks as Mrs. Leeds started to drag J.J. up Deadman's Hill by his ear.

"Man," Adam sighed. "Mrs. Leeds really is a witch!"

"For real," Eugene agreed.

Adam almost felt sorry for J.J.—until J.J. hocked a giant loogie right over his shoulder at Adam.

"You guys are going to be sorry for this!" J.J. screamed as Adam jumped out of the way of his spitball. "Dead sorry!"

4

W atch what you're doing, you idiot!" Adam shouted at Eugene. "You almost smashed my fingers again!"

Adam and Eugene were back in Adam's backyard, pitching their tent for tent night. The problem was, Eugene had the hammer, and he was smashing everything in sight but the tent spikes.

"It's not my fault," Eugene said. "How am I supposed to hit the spikes if you don't hold them steady?"

"I can't hold them steady," Adam said. "Not when you keep smashing my hands!"

"Yeah, well, thanks to you, this whole tent is going to be lopsided," Eugene complained.

Eugene was right. By the time they were done pounding the spikes and stretching their tarps, their tepee-shaped tent looked more like a rectangle.

"Who cares what it looks like," Adam said, trying to avoid another tent-building fight. "At least the stupid thing is up. And we're actually going to get to sleep out tonight."

"Oh, man." Eugene cringed. "Wait until everyone hears that we met Mrs. Leeds in person. They're all going to freak."

"For real," Adam agreed. "And wait until Dougie finds out that you actually took off your sneakers to climb Deadman's Hill. He's going to die laughing."

"He is not," Eugene insisted. "Dougie's just as afraid of the Beast as I am."

"Yeah, right," Adam said. "Dougie's *real* afraid of the Beast."

Just then, an unearthly cry ripped through the air.

Eugene was so startled, he almost hit *himself* with the hammer.

Adam started to laugh, especially when a howling

creature with matted black hair tore across the lawn, heading straight for Eugene.

A moment later, the creature attacked.

"Get off me, you stupid little yippy dog!" Eugene shouted as he pushed Stacey Leeds's dog away from his face.

"Don't be mean to Itsy, Eugene," Stacey hollered as she and Chris Parker walked toward Adam and Eugene. "Itsy loves you," she told Eugene. "Don't you, Itsy?"

Itsy let out a yip, then licked Eugene *splat* on the nose.

"Oh, gross!" Eugene pushed Itsy again. "I don't want Itsy to love me. I hate this stupid dog."

Stacey laughed as she reached down to scoop up her dog.

"Can't you ever leave that mutt at home?" Eugene fussed.

"No," Stacey answered. "Itsy and I do everything together, don't we, Itsy?"

Itsy let out another yip.

"Hey," Chris blurted. "What the heck happened to your tent?"

"What do you mean?" Adam asked her.

"It's all lopsided," Chris said, pointing out the obvious.

Adam shot Eugene a look.

"We built it that way on purpose," Eugene lied. "So we have more room inside."

"What are you going to do in there, Eugene—decorate again?" Stacey teased him.

Chris started to laugh. "Remember when he tried to put carpet in there last year so he wouldn't have to sleep on the ground?" she reminded Stacey.

Stacey and Adam cracked up.

While Eugene liked the *idea* of sleeping out, he really hated roughing it. If Eugene had his way, he and Adam would have pitched their tent inside Adam's room—right over the bunk beds.

"I don't know what's so funny about that," Eugene huffed. "If you cover the ground, the worms and the creepy crawlers can't get to you."

"So let me ask you something." Stacey grinned. "Did you build your port-a-potty this year?"

Adam laughed even harder.

"You wouldn't think it was so hysterical if *you'd* gotten poison ivy all over *your* butt!" Eugene snapped.

"Hey, Eugene!" another voice interrupted. It was Dougie Dembrowski. He and Travis Cook were headed into Adam's yard, too. "Look what I've got," he said, waving what looked like a fat, hairy stick out in front of him. "It's the Beast of Baskerville's leg!"

"Get out of here," Eugene sneered. Even he wasn't gullible enough to believe that—until Dougie waved the leg in his face.

Eugene let out a scream.

Stacey and Chris shrieked.

Itsy let out a yip.

And Adam jumped back.

Dougie really did have a beast's leg in his hands. It was hairy and hoofed.

"Get it away from me!" Eugene cried out in terror. "Get it away!"

Travis cracked up. "Oh, man," he said to Dougie. "You got them good!"

"What the heck is that thing?" Stacey cringed.

"It's the Beast of Baskerville's leg," Dougie repeated.

35

"It is not," Adam said impatiently.

"Is too," Dougie insisted. "And it's filled with his blood!" Dougie pulled what looked like a cork from the top of the leg. Then he opened his mouth and poured a thick red liquid down his throat.

Eugene grabbed his gut like he was about to puke.

And everyone else looked sick—including Itsy.

"It's a flask, you idiots," Travis finally confessed. "And it's filled with tomato juice."

"Why'd you tell them?" Dougie nudged Travis hard.

"What the heck is a flask?" Chris asked, still looking grossed out.

"You know those barrel-shaped things St. Bernards wear around their necks?" Dougie started to explain. "That's a flask. You use it for water or juice when you're hiking or camping. This one came from Venezuela," he went on. "It's a hollowed-out part of a cow's leg. My dad brought it back from a business trip. Pretty cool, huh?"

"Pretty gross," Stacey said, wrinkling her nose.

Chris and Itsy agreed, but Eugene was still too busy gagging to offer an opinion.

"Can I see it?" Adam asked.

"Sure," Dougie said, handing it over.

Adam couldn't help being intrigued by the flask, even as he was repelled by it. It felt hard and hairy, like the limb of a real animal. "Venezuelan people really drink out of cow legs?" he asked.

"I guess." Dougie shrugged.

Eugene was still gagging.

Adam handed the cow leg back to Dougie. "It's a good thing you didn't bring the flask over to Deadman's Hill this morning," he told Dougie. "Eugene would have had a heart attack."

"You guys were on Deadman's Hill?" Travis looked stunned.

"Well, *I* was on Deadman's Hill," Adam said. "Eugene was down in the street taking his sneakers off."

Dougie tried to hide the grin that was spreading from ear to ear.

"What were you doing on Deadman's Hill?" Stacey wanted to know.

"I went to tell J.J. I wasn't coming to his birthday party tonight," Adam answered.

"You what?" Dougie scowled. "Are you out of your

mind? I thought we agreed we just weren't going to show up so that the little creep didn't find out about tent night."

"My mother made me go," Adam told him. "And I didn't say a word about the rest of you guys. Besides, J.J.'s not having a birthday party anymore. At least that's what Mrs. Leeds said."

"You saw Mrs. Leeds?" Dougie's jaw dropped.

Everyone looked stunned. Everyone but Eugene. He still looked green.

"Yeah," Adam said, nodding triumphantly. "She was *out*side!"

"Get out!" Chris said. "What did she look like?"

"She looks like a witch," Adam told them. "She looks pretty old, too. But I couldn't see her face clearly, because she was wearing some kind of net thing over her head."

"Was it an oxygen mask?" Travis wanted to know. "She's allergic to the air or something, isn't she?"

They all rolled their eyes, even Eugene.

"No," Adam said. "It was some kind of veil."

"So what did she say?" Chris asked.

"She said that J.J. wasn't having a party," Adam repeated.

"Yeah," Eugene piped up. "And she ripped up his invitations and threw his elephant cake across the street."

"J.J. had an elephant cake?" Dougie laughed.

"Yup," Eugene said. "It matched his goofy invitations."

"And get this," Adam couldn't resist adding. "She even threatened to call the cops on us!"

"For what?" Chris asked.

"She said she was going to tell them we were 'Beast of Baskerville trespassers,'" Eugene explained.

"Yeah, well, guess what?" Dougie said, grinning devilishly again. "Tonight nobody's going to have to trespass on Mrs. Leeds's property to see the Beast."

Eugene's eyes went wide. "What do you mean?"

"The Beast is going to be hunting for flesh all over the neighborhood tonight," Dougie told him.

"Oh, please," Adam groaned. "Haven't you tortured Eugene enough for one day?"

"I'm serious," Dougie said. "Don't you know what tonight is?"

Eugene shook his head.

"It's the anniversary of the night that *every* kid in Baskerville got eaten by the Beast," Dougie said.

"You're full of cow dung," Adam insisted.

"Am not," Dougie shot back. "It happened the same year my father's great-great-great-grandfather got eaten." He looked straight at Eugene. "Mark my words," he said. "Before the night is through, one of us will be face-to-face with the Beast—and he's definitely going to be hungry."

5

By the time the sun went down and tent night began, Eugene was a Baskerville basket case.

Thanks to Dougie's "anniversary" story, Eugene was convinced that the Beast was out and about, hunting for flesh. He was sure that every kid in the neighborhood was going to get eaten, especially since tent night was going to make them such easy targets.

Adam tried to convince Eugene that Dougie was just trying to scare him again, but Eugene refused to believe him. Instead of dragging in a carpet this year, he dragged in an entire arsenal of weapons. By the time Eugene had finished, they had six baseball bats, three golf clubs, two tent spikes, one hammer, four flashlights, and a Phillips-head screwdriver.

Adam wanted to tell Eugene that his weapons were useless—unless, of course, the Beast wanted to play ball, build a tent, or screw something in under a spotlight. But Adam wasn't about to fuel Eugene's insanity. So he assured Eugene instead that his weapons would ward off the worst.

It took Adam forever to calm Eugene down. And it took him even longer to convince Eugene to sneak out of the yard at ten o'clock, when everyone was supposed to meet at the edge of the neighborhood, down by the woods, across from the old deserted railroad tracks.

The only reason Eugene finally agreed to go was because he didn't want to stay in the tent by himself. Still, he refused to leave without bringing a bat and a flashlight.

By the time they actually made their way around the neighborhood and down to Hollow Lane, the street between the woods and the railroad tracks, everyone was already waiting for them.

"Where have you guys been?" Chris snapped.

"We were just about to come looking for you," Stacey added as Itsy yipped.

Dee-Dee Dunne shook her head. "We were not," she said, reaching into her box of Bugles. "We were going to start without you."

"Yeah," Vanessa Ford echoed. "We were just about to start without you."

Dee-Dee and Vanessa were best friends. They were constantly repeating one another's words, as if they shared one brain. The only thing they didn't share was food. Dee-Dee ate all of that.

"What's with the bat?" Rob Thompson asked Eugene. "I thought we were playing kick the can."

"We are," Eric Green confirmed. "Jay's got the cans."

"They're right here," Jay Reeder said, holding up two soda cans. Jay was Rob and Eric's other best friend. The three of them were sharing a tent in Jay's backyard.

"Hey, Eugene," Dougie teased. "Good thing you brought that bat. That way, when the Beast strikes, you can smash his head in."

Travis stood beside Dougie, smirking.

"Cut it out." Adam elbowed Dougie. "It took me all night to get him here," he whispered.

Dougie smiled impishly. "Want some Beast blood?" He held his cow leg out to Eugene.

Eugene gagged yet again.

"Are we going to play this stupid game or what?" Shauna Larson huffed. Next to her, her spoiled friend Jen Hilton made the same impatient face.

"Calm down," Dougie told them. "We're playing, okay?"

"So how many of us are there?" Travis asked.

Adam counted heads quickly. "Thirteen," he answered.

"Cool," Rob jumped in. "That means odd man is it."

"And who's the odd man?" Stacey smirked. "You?"

"No," Rob shot back. "We're going to draw straws."

"We don't have any straws," Jay informed them.

"We can shoot odds and evens," Eric suggested. "Then we'll narrow it down. The last one to lose will be it."

The rest of the group agreed. The problem was, the

odds-even shoot narrowed down to Eugene and Dee-Dee. Dee-Dee won.

"Hah!" she exclaimed triumphantly, cramming another handful of Bugles into her mouth. "Eugene's it!"

"I'm not doing it," Eugene told Adam under his breath. "No way I'm standing out in this street by myself while everyone else goes and hides."

"You have to," Adam whispered back. "You lost fair and square. Now you have to be it!"

"Does everyone know the rules of the game before we begin?" Dougie's voice interrupted them.

Everyone nodded. But Dougie recited the rules anyway.

"When Eugene starts counting, you've got thirty seconds to hide," he started. "Then Eugene will come looking for you. If he sees you, he has to tap the can three times on the ground. He'll call out your name and your hiding spot. Once you're caught, you're Eugene's prisoner, and you have to go stand near the can. The only way you can escape is if someone else kicks the can. Got it?"

Everyone nodded again.

"Does anybody have a cell phone on them?" Dougie asked.

"*Nooooo*," everyone groaned in unison.

It was rule number one—no phones allowed. Texting made cheating way too easy.

"If anybody gets caught with a phone, you're out for the night," Dougie reminded them.

"We know," Adam said, anxious to move things along.

"Okay, then," Dougie continued. "If Eugene catches everyone, the last prisoner is it. If he doesn't, Eugene has to be it again."

"Here you go, Eugene." Jay handed him the cans.

"Let's do it!" Dougie said. "But be careful out there—the Beast may be joining us." He gave Eugene a wicked smile. Then he and everyone else took off like a shot.

Some of the kids ran toward the railroad tracks and the trestle. Others headed across the street and disappeared into the woods.

Adam followed Stacey, Itsy, and Chris. The four of them hid behind the old water tower, about a hundred feet from the street, on the side of the railroad tracks.

They hid for what seemed like an eternity before Stacey finally spoke up. "What the heck is he doing out there?" she whispered, peeking around the tower at Eugene. "Look at him. He's not even counting or anything. He's just standing there with his bat."

"Not for real," Adam groaned, peeking around the tower, too.

Eugene was cowering under the streetlight, clutching his baseball bat as if he was ready to swing. His head was rotating from side to side. But he wasn't looking for prisoners. He was looking for the Beast.

The other troops started to get restless, too.

"Hey, Eugene!" Eric's voice called out from the woods. "What are you doing? We've been out here for like thirty minutes already! Are you going to try to catch us or what?"

"Yes, I'm going to catch you," Eugene yelled back. "As soon as you come out where I can see you!"

A collective moan rolled across both sides of the street.

"The game doesn't work that way, you yo-yo!" another voice called out. It was Rob's.

"It does when I'm it!" Eugene shouted. "No way I'm stepping out of this light."

"Why not?" Dee-Dee and Vanessa screeched at the same time. "What are you, afraid?"

"You bet I am," Eugene declared. "And you should be, too. The Beast of Baskerville is out tonight! And he's probably right behind you!"

Dee-Dee and Vanessa let out bloodcurdling screams as laughter echoed from both sides of the street.

Eugene started swinging his bat wildly.

But Adam stood frozen, watching in horror as a hideous creature crept out of the shadows.

Eugene was wrong. Dee-Dee and Vanessa were safe. But there was definitely a beast sneaking up behind Eugene.

6

As he saw the creature approaching, Adam tore out from behind the water tower and ran straight for the street. Someone was bound to get hurt. But it wasn't Eugene.

"J.J., look out!" Adam shouted as Eugene swung his bat like a madman.

Luckily, Adam managed to tackle J.J. to the ground before Eugene accidentally bashed his head in.

"Oooooowwwwwccccchhhh!" J.J. cried as he hit the pavement hard.

Adam came crashing down on top of him, knocking the wind out of himself.

A moment later, J.J. knocked the wind out of Adam again when he belted him right in the gut. "Get off me!" he screamed.

"Hey!" Adam shoved J.J. hard as he struggled to catch his breath. "What's the matter with you?"

"What's the matter with *me*?" J.J. snapped. "Look what you did, you idiot!" He held out a bunch of purple party hats. "You smushed my hats!"

"Your what?" Adam snapped back.

"My elephant hats!" J.J. shouted, frantically trying to unsmush them.

"Are you nuts?" Adam asked. "If I hadn't pushed you out of the way, your *head* would have gotten smushed!"

"Yeah, well, you're just lucky it's my birthday," J.J. told him. "Otherwise, I'd kill you for this."

"No way. You just saved the jerk's life, and he's threatening to kill you!" Eugene said, finally lowering his bat.

"Give me that thing." Adam turned his frustration on Eugene. He grabbed the bat from Eugene's hands. "No more weapons for you," he insisted. "Or somebody really is going to get killed."

"What's going on out here?" Travis asked as he and Dougie stepped out of the woods. The moment they saw J.J., they froze in their tracks.

"Oh, no," Dougie groaned, burying his face in his hands. "This can't be real."

"Don't even try to run away from me, Dougie," J.J. said without looking in Dougie's direction. "I know you guys are having tent night. And I know you weren't planning to come to my party!"

Dougie gave Adam a dirty look. "I thought you said you didn't tell him about tent night."

"I didn't!" Adam protested.

"Then how did he know?" Travis asked.

"Because I'm psychic," J.J. announced.

"Yeah, right," Dougie snorted.

From behind the water tower, Itsy started to yip up a storm.

"Come out, come out, wherever you are, Stacey Leeds!" J.J. hollered. "And bring your friend, Chris, with you, too!"

Stacey and Chris headed for the street with Itsy in tow. All three looked totally embarrassed.

A moment later, Shauna and Jen crept into sight. They tried to creep out of it, too, but J.J. had already spotted them.

Rob, Eric, and Jay climbed up from the railroad tracks.

"Oh, no!" Eric gasped loudly. "Booger boy is here!"

Jay elbowed Eric hard—but too late.

"Booger boy, huh?" J.J. growled as he spun toward the three of them. "You're the booger boys."

"Hey!" Dee-Dee's voice rolled out of the woods before she did. "Are we playing this stupid game or what?"

The moment Dee-Dee saw J.J., she jumped.

Vanessa slammed into her back.

"Hi, Dee-Dee." J.J. affected Dee-Dee and Vanessa's obnoxious tones. "Hi, Vanessa."

"Hi, J.J." Dee-Dee and Vanessa looked like a couple of deer caught in headlights. "Sorry about your party," they lied in unison.

"Sure you are," J.J. said. "But now you don't have to worry about missing it. Because I'm bringing the party to you guys. See?" He held out the elephant hats. "I've got party hats for the crowd."

Everyone exchanged horrified looks.

"You've got to be kidding me." Dougie started to laugh.

"No way, he's got purple elephant hats." Eric laughed, too.

"Hey, J.J.," Rob said. "Aren't you a little too old for elephant hats?"

"For real," Shauna and Jen agreed.

"So what are we going to do once we put on our party hats, J.J.?" Dee-Dee sneered. "Play pin the tail on the donkey?"

"I have an idea," Travis jumped in. "We could play pin the tail on J.J.!"

Everyone laughed even harder.

But Adam couldn't help feeling sorry for J.J., especially now that he'd met J.J.'s horrible mother.

"Leave him alone," he said. "It's his birthday, for Pete's sake."

"So who wants a hat?" J.J. asked, oblivious to the teasing.

"Adam will take one, won't you, Adam?" Dougie needled.

"Sure," Adam said, shooting Dougie a dirty look. "I'll take one."

A snicker ran through the crowd.

"Here," J.J. said, holding the hats out to Adam. "You can have any one you want, except the one that says 'Birthday Boy.' That one is mine."

"It ought to say 'Birthday Dweeb,'" Travis whispered loud enough for everyone to hear.

The snicker turned into full-blown laughter.

"You know what?" Adam said, quickly changing his mind. "Give me the hat later," he told J.J. Being nice was one thing, but wearing an elephant hat was another.

"Suit yourself," J.J. said. Then he hocked a big loogie and spit it across the street.

"Ew, gross!" Shauna and Jen cringed at the same time.

"So what are we doing?" Jay moaned. "Are we going to play kick the can or what?"

"Not with the booger boy, we're not," Eric said.

"Yes, we are," Adam said. "We're playing with the booger boy!"

The words slipped out of Adam's mouth before he

realized what he was saying. He gave J.J. an apologetic shrug, but J.J. didn't seem to notice—or care.

"Yeah, well, who's going to be it?" Eric asked. "Because if Eugene goes again, we'll be sitting out here all night."

"I'll be it," Adam offered. It was easier than going through an odds-evens shoot again.

Everyone agreed.

As soon as Adam said "go," they all took off in different directions—mostly away from J.J., who disappeared down by the railroad tracks.

Eugene plunked himself down on the curb.

"What are you doing?" Adam asked.

"Watching," Eugene answered. "No way I'm hiding with the booger boy *and* the Beast on the loose."

"Suit yourself," Adam sighed. Then he closed his eyes and started to count. The moment he reached thirty, he headed for the woods.

"Where are you going?" Eugene cried, springing to his feet and reaching for his flashlight.

"I'm going to look for prisoners," Adam told him.

"Not without me, you're not," Eugene said, turning

on his flashlight. "No way you're leaving me here by myself." He shined the beam of the flashlight in Adam's face.

"Turn that thing off!" Adam quickly covered his charbroiled eyeballs. "This is supposed to be a surprise attack, not a surrender!"

Eugene complied grudgingly.

"Now keep your mouth shut and stay close," Adam ordered.

Like Adam really had to tell Eugene to stay close. By the time they entered the woods, Eugene was stepping on the backs of Adam's sneakers.

"Not that close," Adam huffed, giving Eugene a shove.

"Sorry," Eugene grumbled.

"Keep your eyes out for Dee-Dee," Adam told him as they moved through the trees. "She shouldn't be too hard to spot."

"*You* keep your eyes out for Dee-Dee," Eugene said. "I'm keeping my eyes out for you-know-who."

Just then, a loud clang tore through the air.

"What the heck is that?" Eugene yelped, practically leaping onto Adam's back.

"It's the can, you idiot," Adam said. "One of those clowns must have kicked it."

The sound of tin rolling across blacktop continued to echo.

"Yeah, well, they must have kicked it pretty good," Eugene whined.

"Why would somebody do that?" Adam grumbled as he and Eugene headed back to the street. "Nobody's in prison yet."

Just then, another sound filled the air. It wasn't a tinny clang. It was a loud clop.

Actually, it was lots of clops—clops that sounded like hooves pounding against the pavement!

Adam froze in his tracks.

Whatever was moving across the blacktop now was definitely not a can.

7

"Do you hear that?" Eugene shrieked as the clopping sound got closer and closer.

Adam nodded nervously.

"It's the Beast!" Eugene cried. "He's after us!"

Adam was thinking the very same thing. But he wasn't about to admit it, not even to himself. "It's not the Beast," he told Eugene, trying to sound sure of himself.

"Oh, yeah?" Eugene challenged. "Then who's clippity-clopping across the street?"

"I don't know." Adam gulped. "Maybe somebody's

wearing ski boots or something. I mean, ski boots make a lot of noise when you try to run in them on the pavement."

"Ski boots?" Eugene snapped. "It's the middle of summer! Nobody's wearing ski boots!"

Adam didn't need Eugene to tell him just how stupid that suggestion was. He realized it the minute it slipped out of his mouth. But Eugene was determined to cram it back down his throat anyway.

"Let me tell you something, bub," Eugene kept going. "Even if somebody was wearing ski boots, they don't clippity-clop! Only animal hooves clippity-clop. And no one in our neighborhood has a pair of those. No one but the Beast!"

Eugene was ranting so loudly, neither of them noticed that the clopping sound had faded.

A moment later, so did Adam's fears.

Eugene was right. What they'd heard was animal hooves. But the animal wasn't the Beast.

"It's a deer," Adam told Eugene, laughing at himself for being so scared. "You see?" he said, pointing to the shadowy creature darting through the trees. "It was just a stupid deer. There are hundreds of deer out in these woods. And they're always crossing that street."

"Oh, right," Eugene huffed. "Like I'm really supposed to believe that a deer kicked the can."

"Noooooo," Adam said. "The deer crossed the street. Someone else kicked the can."

"Yeah," Eugene insisted, "the Beast."

"Cut me a break," Adam said, shaking his head. "The Beast did not kick the can. Come on," he continued, heading for the street. "I'll prove it to you. Hey guys!" he screamed as he stepped out of the woods. "Everybody get out here now!"

One by one the neighborhood kids slowly made their way to the street.

"What's going on now?" Dougie groaned as he and Travis came into view, followed by Rob, Eric, and Jay.

"You tell me," Adam said to the group as Dee-Dee shoveled a handful of Bugles into her mouth.

"What are you talking about?" Stacey asked.

"The can," Adam said. "Who kicked it?"

Everyone shrugged.

"Well, somebody kicked it," Adam said accusingly. "Because it's halfway down the street!" He pointed to the can.

"Nobody kicked it," Jay said. "Because nobody was in prison."

"No kidding," Adam shot back.

"Hey," Eric chimed in. "Where's the booger boy?"

Adam quickly scanned the group, as did everyone else.

J.J. was nowhere to be seen.

"J.J. must have kicked it," Dougie decided. Then he yelled at the top of his lungs, "Hey, J.J.! Get out here, you little booger ball!"

There was no answer, and no appearance.

"He was hiding by the trestle," Shauna said. "Jen and I saw him down there."

"Hey, J.J.!" Dougie screamed again, crossing the street. "Get up here now, before I come down there and kick *you* in the can!"

There was still no response.

"Let's go scare the daylights out of him," Dougie said.

Adam rolled his eyes, but he followed Dougie and Travis anyway, with Eugene right on his heels, swinging his flashlight.

The rest of the group stayed put.

As the four of them headed down the hill to the trestle, Adam was sure that Dougie was right: J.J. was the can-kicking culprit. And he was just as sure that the little nerd would deny it.

But J.J. had vanished.

"Where is he?" Dougie asked when they reached the trestle.

Travis shrugged. Then Eugene let out a gasp. "Look!" he cried, directing the beam of the flashlight. He wasn't pointing the light toward the trestle. He was pointing it toward the muddy ground a few feet away.

J.J.'s purple elephant hats were scattered all over the place.

"What's your problem?" Adam asked Eugene. "It's just J.J.'s party hats."

"Yeah!" Eugene said. "But look what's right next to them!"

Adam took a step closer. The moment he did, he saw what Eugene was gasping about.

There, in the mud beside the elephant hats, were two sets of hoofprints.

8

Adam bent over to examine the muddy prints.

"Oh, man!" Eugene started to freak. "I told you the Beast was out tonight!" he snapped at Adam. "I told you somebody was going to get eaten! But you just wouldn't listen to me, would you?"

"Calm down," Adam said to Eugene. "The Beast is not out tonight. And nobody got eaten."

"Oh, yeah? Then where's J.J.? And who left these footprints?" Eugene asked.

"They're deer prints, you idiot!" Adam practically shouted. "I told you, deer are all over the place out here."

He turned to Dougie for support. "Will you please tell him that these are deer prints?"

But he should have known Dougie wasn't going to let an opportunity like this one slide by. "Oh, I don't know, Adam," he said, feigning fear. "These prints look awfully big to be deer prints."

"For real." Travis backed Dougie up. "They look like the Beast's prints to me."

"Cut me a break," Adam groaned. "How do you know what the Beast's prints look like?"

"I, uh . . ." Travis stammered, trying to come up with an answer. He looked to Dougie for another good story.

"My father's great-great-great-grandfather took an imprint of the Beast's hooves," Dougie piped up. "And my grandfather still has it. Travis saw it when we were visiting him last year."

"That's right." Travis nodded. "That's where I saw it."

These guys are too much, Adam thought. "Your father's triple-great-grandfather took an imprint of the Beast's hooves?" he repeated incredulously.

Dougie nodded.

"Was that before or after he got eaten?" Adam challenged.

"Uh-duh," Dougie said. "Before."

Adam shook his head in disgust. Dougie wasn't about to give in.

"I'm getting out of here!" Eugene exclaimed. "Before you-know-who shows up again!" He took off running for the street.

Dougie and Travis cracked up.

"You guys are such jerks," Adam huffed. "You're scaring him half to death!"

"I know," Dougie said. "It's great!"

"No, it's not great," Adam told him. "Because I'm the one who's going to have to deal with him all night." He took off after Eugene.

Dougie and Travis followed, laughing.

The moment Eugene hit the street, he started to babble. "The Beast ate J.J.!" he announced to the rest of the group in a panic. "His elephant hats are all over the place down there. And so are the Beast's footprints!"

"Yeah, right," Eric snickered.

"I'm serious!" Eugene shouted. "The Beast ate the booger ball!"

Everyone cracked up, including Itsy, who yipped up a storm.

"You're out of your mind," Rob told Eugene. "There's no way anybody would eat the booger ball—not even the Beast."

"Yeah, well, he did," Eugene insisted as Dougie and Travis joined the group. "Tell him, Dougie."

Dougie and Travis exchanged glances. "Could be," Dougie said, smirking. "J.J. *is* missing, and there *are* some pretty big hoofprints down there," he informed the group.

"They're *deer* prints!" Adam had had it. "Big, stupid deer prints!"

"Oh, yeah?" Travis said. "What about the party hats? No way J.J. would let go of those."

"Not unless he was fighting for his life," Dougie added.

Eugene gulped.

"And he definitely wouldn't be fighting for his life against a deer," Dougie concluded.

"Cut it out, Dougie," Stacey snapped at him. "It's not funny anymore."

"I'm not trying to be funny," Dougie said. "I'm just trying to figure out what happened to J.J."

"He probably went home because everyone was picking on him," Adam decided. "And he probably ditched his party hats because none of us would wear them."

"Adam's right," Chris agreed. "We were pretty mean to him."

"Oh, please," Dee-Dee growled. "Like there's any way to be nice to that creep."

"For real," Vanessa said.

"But it *is* his birthday," Shauna chimed in. "We could have at least *pretended* to be nice to him."

"It's a little too late for that now!" Eugene was still in a frenzy. "The little booger ball is dead!"

"He is not dead," Adam insisted. "He's home. If you want to, we can all go over there and I'll prove it to you."

Everyone stared at him.

"Are you out of your mind?" Eric asked. "No way I'm climbing Deadman's Hill in the middle of the night to look for a booger ball."

No one else wanted to go, either, especially Eugene.

"I say we forget about the little creep," Dee-Dee suggested. "We can be nice to him next year."

"Yeah," Eugene said, "*if* he's still alive."

Adam rolled his eyes in exasperation.

"So are we playing kick the can or what?" Jay finally wanted to know.

"We're in," Dougie answered for himself and Travis.

"Us, too," Dee-Dee and Vanessa said.

"Rob and I are playing," Eric informed the group.

"We're playing, too," Stacey told them as Itsy and Chris nodded yes.

"And what about you guys?" Jay asked Adam.

"We're playing," Adam said as Eugene shook his head no.

"Good. You're still it," Rob announced, handing Adam the can. "Whoever kicked this thing dented it pretty good," he told Adam. "You want to use the other one?"

"No," Adam said. "This one's okay." He set it down in the middle of the street, then hollered, "Go."

Once again, everyone but Eugene took off.

After he had counted to thirty, Adam headed for the woods, with Eugene right behind him.

A moment later, someone kicked the can again—someone who definitely wasn't out to play games.

9

T hat's it!" Adam declared as he stormed toward the street with Eugene clinging to the back of his shirt. "I've had it with Dougie. I swear I'm going to cram that can right up his nose!"

"How do you know it was Dougie?" Eugene asked, trying to hold Adam back. "How do you know it *wasn't* the Beast?"

Adam groaned as he kept tugging Eugene forward. He was sure that the moment they stepped out of the woods, they'd catch Dougie red-footed, trying to run from the scene of the crime.

But Dougie was nowhere in sight, not even after Adam forced the rest of the group to resurface again.

"Doug-gie!" Adam screamed at the top of his lungs as he picked up the can from the street. It was totally smashed. "Get out here, you jerk! And bring Travis with you!"

Everyone waited. But Dougie didn't appear.

Neither did Travis.

Eugene jumped to the obvious conclusion—at least the conclusion that was obvious to him. "The Beast got them," he announced to the group. "Dougie and Travis got eaten like J.J. And the Beast smashed our can."

"The Beast did not smash our can!" Adam snapped. "Dougie and Travis are just trying to freak us out."

"Yeah, well, they're doing a pretty good job of it," Shauna gulped.

Thanks to Dougie's disappearing act and the mutilated can, Eugene's panic was becoming contagious. Within seconds, half the group was infected.

"Maybe Eugene is right," Jen said. "Maybe the Beast really is out tonight."

Adam sighed in exasperation. "It's bad enough that

Eugene's a basket case. Don't you guys bug out on me, too. I'm telling you, Dougie's just fooling around."

"I don't know," Dee-Dee said. "This isn't like Dougie. I mean, if Dougie really were trying to freak us out, he'd be up here doing it in our faces."

"Dee-Dee's right," Jay agreed. "Dougie wouldn't want to miss out on the chance to see Eugene having a nervous breakdown."

"So what are you saying?" Adam stared at Jay. "That *you* think the Beast ate them, too?"

"Noooooooo." Jay rolled his eyes. "I just think it's weird, that's all."

"It's not weird," Stacey chimed in. "It's Dougie. He and Travis will do anything to torture Eugene. They're probably hiding somewhere, laughing their butts off."

"I'm with Stacey," Rob added.

"Me too," Chris said.

Itsy yipped her agreement.

"Did anyone see them before the can got smashed?" Adam asked.

"Yeah." Eric nodded. "It looked like they were headed for the sewer pipe down near the trestle."

"How much you want to bet that's where they're hiding now?" Adam was sure of it. "Come on," he said, "let's check it out."

"No way!" Shauna refused to budge. "I'm not going down near that trestle. That's where J.J. got eaten!"

"I'm not going, either," Jen said, plunking herself down on the curb next to Shauna. "We'll wait right here."

"Fine," Adam groaned. "Just keep your eyes out for Dougie and Travis. If you see them, cram this can up Dougie's nose." Adam tossed the smushed can to Jen. "What about you?" he asked, turning to Eugene. "Are you coming?"

"Are you guys going?" Eugene asked the rest of the group.

Everyone nodded.

"Then there's no way I'm staying up here with these two," Eugene said.

"Why not?" Shauna sounded offended.

"Because there's safety in numbers," Eugene replied.

Shauna laughed. "Yeah, right," she said.

"There is," Eugene insisted. "And if you had half a brain, you'd come with us."

"I don't think so," Jen said.

"Suit yourself," Eugene shot back. Then he hurried after Adam as his friend led the rest of the group down the hill toward the trestle.

The moment they got there, Eugene let out a scream.

"What?" Adam was startled out of his wits, along with everyone else.

"Look!" Eugene cried, pointing the flashlight toward the ground. "The elephant hats are gone!"

"Sooooo?" Dee-Dee said. "What's that supposed to mean?"

"I don't know," Eugene answered. "But it can't be good."

Adam was just about to tell him to shut up when Eric spoke up.

"Give it a rest, will you, Eugene?" Eric snapped. "I bet Dougie took the hats."

"For what?" Eugene wanted to know.

"How do I know?" Eric said. "Maybe he and Travis are throwing a party for themselves in the sewer."

Adam had to laugh. Eugene was gnawing away at everyone's nerves.

"Let's just find them, okay?" Stacey barked before Itsy joined in.

The group followed Adam as he crossed over the railroad tracks under the trestle. Eugene was still bringing up the rear, swinging his flashlight around. They headed for the giant sewer pipe.

"I can't believe those idiots would actually hide in this pipe," Dee-Dee said as they crowded around the opening. "It's disgusting."

"It sure is," Vanessa agreed. She covered her nose.

The sewer pipe was at least five feet in diameter and smelled to high heaven. Adam was having a hard time just getting close to the thing. And it was so black inside, he could barely see more than a foot into the tube.

"Are they in there?" Eric asked, struggling to get by Dee-Dee.

"I can't see," Adam said.

"Yo, Dougie!" Rob shouted. "We know you're in there, so you might as well come out."

The only response was the sound of dripping water echoing through the pipe.

"Hey, Eugene," Adam said over his shoulder. "Give me your flashlight, will you?"

"No way!" Eugene told him.

"Then get over here and shine it down this pipe!" Adam ordered.

Eugene pushed his way past Eric to get up beside Adam. He directed the beam of the flashlight into the murky blackness.

"Do you see them?" Stacey wanted to know.

Adam shook his head. All he could see was the slimy walls of the tunnel and the black sludge that lined the bottom.

If Dougie and Travis were in there, they were definitely out of the spotlight.

"Come on, Dougie!" Adam's voice bounced off the walls. "Enough is enough already! Get out here!"

There was still no response.

"You see?" Eugene said anxiously. "They're not in the sewer. They're down in the bowels of the Beast!"

"Shut up already!" Adam lost his patience. "Give me that thing," he said, grabbing the flashlight from Eugene's hand.

"What are you doing?" Eugene yelped.

"I'm going to prove to you once and for all what an idiot you're being," Adam answered as he stepped into the pipe.

"You're not really going in there, are you?" Eric asked.

Adam nodded. "Now who wants to come with me?"

No one volunteered—not even Itsy.

"Fine," Adam said. "I'll go by myself."

As he took another step forward, he pulled the neck of his T-shirt up over his nose. The stench outside the pipe was bad enough, but *inside,* it was deadly. Adam's stomach crawled up his throat. He didn't even want to think about *what* he was smelling.

He didn't want to look down, either. Especially since the soles of his sneakers kept landing in piles of squishy wet gunk.

"Hey, Dougie," Adam called out as he kept his eyes focused ahead. "You might as well give it up. I'm coming to get you."

The only reply was the echo of Adam's own voice.

Behind him, the opening at the end of the tunnel

was getting farther and farther away, as were the faces of his friends.

Adam's nerves were beginning to fray. Being in the sewer pipe was starting to feel an awful lot like being buried alive. What if it collapsed on his head? Or what if everybody in the neighborhood flushed at the same time? What then?

That thought was way too disgusting to bear.

"Dougie!" Adam shouted nervously. "When I get you, you're dead. Do you hear me?"

Just then, a horrible growl filled the tunnel. It was loud and deep, almost unearthly. And it was coming from up ahead, around the curve in the pipe.

Adam froze in his tracks.

Someone was hiding down in the sewer—but it didn't sound anything like Dougie.

10

Adam's heart was pounding so furiously, he could hear it echoing off the walls of the tunnel.

"Get out of there, Adam!" Eugene screamed hysterically into the pipe. "It's the Beast!"

Adam turned to make a run for it. But the sludge under his feet had already slimed the treads on his sneakers. He started to slip.

He tried to brace himself against one of the walls, but the foul-smelling gunk lining the sides of the pipe was just as slimy as the sludge on its bottom.

Before Adam could stop himself, he fell *splat* into a puddle of squishy black goo.

Luckily, he landed on his butt.

But he didn't stay on it for long.

Adam was up and running for the exit two seconds later.

By the time he managed to slide through the mouth of the pipe, the growling had stopped.

As soon as Adam was on solid ground, he doubled over to catch his breath.

Eugene tugged him forward frantically. "Come on! We've got to get out of here!"

"Calm down," Adam said. Now that he was out of the sewer pipe, what he'd heard inside it seemed much less frightening.

"Calm down?" Eugene shrieked. "Are you out of your mind? The Beast is in there!"

"It's not the Beast," Adam assured him, coming up with a logical explanation for what they'd heard. "It was Travis."

"What do you mean it was Travis?" Dee-Dee gulped as she choked on a Bugle. "There was growling in there!"

"Yeah." Adam nodded. "But it wasn't the Beast."

"Travis doesn't growl," Jay said.

"No, but he burps real good," Adam told them.

They all looked confused.

"Travis can burp the entire alphabet in four breaths," Adam reminded his friends.

"What are you saying?" Stacey looked at Adam skeptically. "That the growling inside the pipe was Travis burping?"

"Yup," Adam confirmed. "That's exactly what I'm saying."

"Did you see Travis?" Eric wanted to know.

"No," Adam answered. "But listen." He stuck his head inside the pipe. Then he pulled up the air from his gut and let one rip.

"Brrrrrrruuuuuuuuuuuurrrrrrrrrrp!"

The sound bouncing off the walls of the pipe really did sound like a growl. It was nowhere near as frightening as the sound they'd heard before, but it was enough to sway everyone—everyone but Eugene.

"I don't care what you guys say," Eugene insisted. "The Beast is in that sewer pipe. And I'm getting out of here." He grabbed the flashlight from Adam's hand. Then he tore over the railroad tracks and ran for the hill.

A moment later, he was screaming bloody murder.

"Now what?" Adam sighed in frustration.

"Who knows," Eric groaned. "Maybe he bumped into his own shadow."

Adam started to laugh.

But Eugene continued to scream.

"Maybe we should go check on him," Stacey suggested.

"Why?" Vanessa asked. "Shauna and Jen are up there. Let them deal with him."

"Yeah, well, if they don't deal with him soon, he's going to wake up the entire neighborhood," Jay said. "And if somebody calls the cops on us, we're all going to be in serious trouble."

"Aw, man." Eric cringed at the thought. "My mother will kill me if she finds out we're not in our tent. She'll never let me sleep out again."

"Tell me about it," Rob commiserated. "My parents will ground me for life if they know we're roaming the streets at this hour!"

Adam didn't even want to think about what his parents would do. "Don't worry about it," he told the group as he tried not to panic over the parent problem himself. "There's no way anybody's going to hear Eugene screaming. The woods across the street are too deep."

"Are you kidding me?" Dee-Dee snapped. "He's screaming loud enough to wake up Japan!"

"Why don't you just go get him," Eric suggested.

"Fine," Adam huffed, heading for the hill.

"Wait up!" Stacey called after him. "We'll go with you."

Adam turned to see Stacey, Itsy, and Chris rushing to catch up.

The rest of the group stayed put.

"I swear I'm going to kill him for this," Adam muttered as he reached the street. He was just about to, too—until he saw why Eugene was screaming.

"What's his problem?" Chris wanted to know as she slammed into Adam's back.

Adam didn't have to answer. The answer was clear.

It was lying in the middle of the street—in a puddle that looked like blood.

11

Stacey gasped so loudly that Itsy started to bark.

Eugene spun toward the sound, looking terrified.

Adam and Chris stood frozen.

"He got them!" Eugene cried, pointing to the remains in the street. "The Beast got Shauna and Jen!"

Adam swallowed hard as Stacey and Chris exchanged horrified looks.

"I told them there was safety in numbers!" Eugene continued to freak. "But they didn't want to listen to me, did they? Nooooooooooo," he ranted. "They wanted to stay up here like a couple of sitting ducks. And now they're duck soup! You see," he said, pointing to the remains. "That's all that's left of them. One lousy shoe and a hair clip."

"Stop yelling," Adam told Eugene, trying to keep a level head. There had to be a logical explanation for Shauna and Jen's disappearance. Adam had the sneaking suspicion it had something to do with Dougie. "Did you see Shauna and Jen when you got up here?" he asked.

"No," Eugene answered, "just what's left of them."

"That *is* Shauna's sneaker," Stacey told Adam, crouching down to get a better look.

"And that's definitely Jen's clip," Chris pointed out.

"And they're both lying in a puddle of blood!" Eugene added hysterically.

"Why would one sneaker and a hair clip be lying in a puddle of blood?" Adam wondered aloud. It just didn't make any sense.

"I'll tell you why." Eugene's brain was spinning out of control. "Because the Beast burped them up—*after* he ate them!"

Stacey and Chris cringed at the thought.

"Five minutes ago, you thought the Beast was down

in the sewer pipe," Adam snapped nervously at Eugene. "How could he have been in two places at the same time?"

"Who knows," Eugene said. "Maybe that pipe has another opening. Maybe when you ran out one way, the Beast ran out the other."

Eugene's probably right, Adam thought. *There probably is more than one opening in that pipe. But it wasn't the Beast who sneaked out. It was Dougie and Travis.*

"How much you want to bet that puddle isn't blood," Adam told Eugene, suddenly remembering Dougie's tomato-juice-filled cow leg.

"Are you blind?" Eugene asked. "Or just stupid? Look at that stuff. Of course it's blood."

"Is not," Adam said. "It's tomato juice."

"Tomato juice?" Stacey repeated, sounding confused.

"From Dougie's cow leg," Adam told her.

"But you said Dougie was in the pipe," Chris reminded him.

"He was," Adam said. "But I guarantee you Eugene's right. There *is* another opening in that pipe. And I'll bet you anything Dougie and Travis sneaked out of there to

87

come up here and get Shauna and Jen to play along with their prank."

.   "Oh, really?" Eugene wasn't buying it. "Well, if that's tomato juice, why don't you just stick your finger in that puddle and taste it?" he dared Adam.

"No way!" Adam told him. "I'm not licking up dirty tomato juice. Especially since Shauna's stinky sneaker is sitting in it. If you're so worried about it, why don't you taste it?" he challenged.

"Oh, I'm worried about it all right," Eugene said. "Because that's not tomato juice!" he shouted. "Why don't you just get it through your fat head that the Beast is out having himself a smorgasbord tonight! And Shauna and Jen are history, pal—just like Dougie and Travis and J.J.!"

"They are not!" Adam shouted back. "And I'll prove it to you!"

"Fine," Eugene yelled. "Lick up the blood. But when you start puking, I don't want to hear about it!"

With all the courage he could muster, Adam bent over to stick his finger into what he hoped really was a puddle of tomato juice. He had no idea what a puddle of blood would feel like, but he imagined it would be sticky. Luckily, this wasn't.

"Whew," Adam sighed as he pulled his finger from the wet pavement.

"You're not really going to taste that, are you?" Stacey winced.

Adam nodded. What choice did he have? If he didn't lick his finger, Eugene would never shut up.

Please let this be tomato juice, Adam thought as he slowly lifted his hand to his mouth. He was about to touch the tip of his finger to the tip of his tongue when something horrifying drifted out of the woods.

Adam let his hand drop to his side.

There was no point in taking the taste test now.

12

"Aaaaaaaaaaaaaaaaggghhhh!"

Shauna and Jen's terrified screams filled the air. "Help us, Eugene!" they cried in their best horror-movie voices. "The Beast is after us!"

Adam shot Eugene a look. "Shauna and Jen are dead, huh?" he said, wiping his finger on the side of his shorts. "Then how come they're screaming?"

"Okay." Eugene gave in just an inch. "Maybe they're not dead. Maybe they're running around those woods like a couple of headless chickens trying to escape from being dead. Didn't you hear them? The Beast is after them!"

Adam laughed.

Stacey started to laugh, too.

"Listen, Eugene," Chris said. "If the Beast really is chasing Shauna and Jen through the woods, why don't they run for the street?"

"Adam's right," Stacey chimed in. "Shauna and Jen are just playing along with Dougie and Travis."

The sound of laughter suddenly punctuated the point. It was coming from the woods.

"Very funny, Dougie," Adam shouted toward the trees. "You guys are a real laugh riot."

There was no response.

"I don't think that was Dougie," Eugene said nervously.

"No, Eugene," Adam mocked. "It was the Beast. The Beast is laughing at us now," he said, rolling his eyes.

"I can't believe what jerks those guys are being," Stacey complained. "We were all supposed to be having a good time tonight, not just Dougie and Travis."

"For real," Chris agreed.

"So what do you want to do now?" Stacey asked Adam.

"I don't know," Adam answered. He had no desire to spend the rest of the night being tortured by Dougie and Travis.

Just then, the rest of the group made its way up from the railroad tracks. Eric was out in front.

"Hey, Adam," he called from the top of the hill. "If Dougie and Travis are in that pipe, they're not coming out."

"They're already out," Adam informed him. "There must be another opening," he explained, "because they're in the woods now."

"You're kidding me," Jay said.

"No," Stacey told him. "And they're out there with Shauna and Jen."

"Hey!" Dee-Dee gasped as the gang hit the street. "What's with all this blood?"

"Oh, man!" Vanessa looked sick. "Whose sneaker is that?"

"It's Shauna's," Adam answered. "And it's not blood," he told Dee-Dee. "It's tomato juice. Dougie and Travis have Shauna and Jen playing Beast pranks now, too."

"Terrific," Eric groaned. "So I guess we're not playing kick the can anymore, are we?"

"No," Adam said. "It looks like we're playing the Dougie-Is-a-Stupid-Jerk game the rest of the night."

"Yeah, well, I'm not playing," Dee-Dee said. "No way I'm waiting around for those guys to show their faces again. Come on," she told Vanessa. "Let's go back to our tent and eat those cupcakes my mom baked for us."

"You already ate them," Vanessa pointed out.

"Oh, right," Dee-Dee remembered. "Well, then, let's go eat the cookies. See you clowns later," Dee-Dee said as she and Vanessa headed down the street.

"So what do you guys want to do?" Adam asked Rob, Eric, and Jay.

"I say we go find those four jerks and play kick the can with their butts," Eric suggested.

"Sounds like a good plan to me," Adam agreed.

"For real," Rob and Jay said together.

Stacey and Chris were up for some "can-kicking," too, as was Itsy.

Eugene, however, made his own suggestion.

"I say we all go home and lock ourselves in before the Beast starts looking for dessert," he told the group.

"Come on, Eugene," Adam sighed. "Let's at least get even with these guys. We've been planning this night for weeks."

"Yeah," Eugene shot back, "and so has the Beast."

"Look," Adam said reasonably, "if we don't find them in the next half hour, we'll all go home, okay?"

"That's if we're all still alive," Eugene grumbled under his breath.

"Why don't we split up and go in different directions?" Eric asked as they moved toward the woods. "That way, we're bound to snag them."

"Good idea," Adam agreed.

"Oh, no," Eugene protested. "No splitting, pal," he said, grabbing Adam's shirttail.

"Not us!" Adam groaned. "Us!" he said, pointing to Eric, Rob, and Jay.

"Geez, oh, man." Eric laughed. "He really is going to have a nervous breakdown, isn't he?"

"Look," Rob said. "We'll take the side that leads out to Merion Place. You guys go left, out toward Penlar."

"That'll work," Adam decided.

"Chris and I will go with you," Stacey told Adam.

As Rob, Eric, and Jay disappeared through the trees to their right, Adam and his gang slipped undercover to the left.

They'd taken only a few steps into the woods when the branches above their heads started to rustle loudly. It sounded as if someone was up in one of the trees, shaking its branches furiously.

Adam stopped dead in his tracks.

"What the heck is that?" Eugene moaned as Stacey, Itsy, and Chris let out startled yips of their own.

Adam looked up expecting to see Dougie and Travis peering down at them. He was sure the two of them were just pulling another Beast prank. . . .

Until Eugene swung the beam of his flashlight upward—and a big hairy creature came into view.

Adam's adrenaline started to pump, even before Eugene announced, "It's the Beast!"

13

Adam watched wide-eyed as the hairy creature above them crept deliberately through the leaves, along the branch, straight down the tree trunk.

"Don't move," Adam whispered to the group, barely forming the words with his lips. The last thing in the world Adam wanted was to be spotted by the beady-eyed beast that was coming toward them.

"If that's the Beast," Stacey whispered to Eugene, "he must be eating some pretty small people." She chuckled.

"Yeah." Chris snickered, too. "Like teeny, tiny, two-inch-tall people," she said.

Adam was pretty amused himself as he watched

the possum scurry across the ground, out of the spotlight.

Itsy started to growl.

"It's okay, Itsy," Stacey told the dog in her arms. "It's just a possum. It's not going to hurt you."

Itsy growled even louder, baring her sharp little teeth.

"What's up with her?" Adam asked.

"I guess the possum must have spooked her," Stacey said.

Itsy started to bark viciously—at least, viciously for Itsy. Then she leaped out of Stacey's arms and tore after the possum.

"Spooked, my butt!" Adam said. "Itsy's trying to catch that thing!"

"Give me that flashlight, Eugene," Stacey demanded, grabbing it from his hands. "Itsy!" she called out as she took off after the dog. "Get over here!"

Adam, Chris, and Eugene followed.

"Itsy never runs away from Stacey," Chris said, sounding concerned.

"Well, maybe Itsy never saw a possum before," Adam suggested.

"I hope that dog's not planning to attack that thing," Eugene said. "Otherwise, there's going to be blood in these woods, too—namely, Itsy's."

"Don't even say that, Eugene." Chris slapped his arm.

"It-sy!" Stacey's cries grew more frantic as she picked up her pace.

Itsy was nowhere to be seen.

"Where is she?" Stacey fretted.

"She can't be too far," Adam said. "I'm sure we'll find her any second now."

"Unless the possum finds her first," Eugene whispered under his breath.

"Shut up, Eugene." Chris heard him anyway.

Just then, Itsy started to bark again. Only this time, she didn't sound very vicious. She was yipping frantically, as if her life was at stake.

"Over here," Adam said, turning toward the sound.

Stacey quickly shone the light in the same direction.

For a moment, Adam was afraid they really were going to see Itsy being attacked by the possum. But the possum was nowhere in sight. Itsy wasn't barking at a creature. She was barking at the ground, and she was shaking like crazy.

"What's the matter, Its?" Stacey said, rushing over to scoop up her dog.

Itsy kept barking.

"Maybe she *smells* the possum," Adam suggested.

"Maybe," Stacey said, shining the flashlight down at her feet. As she did, she let out a gasp.

Itsy had picked up an animal's scent. But it didn't belong to the possum.

14

Don't even say it!" Adam warned Eugene as he stared at the hoofprints on the ground.

Stacey gulped.

So did Chris.

"It's not the Beast," Adam told them. "I've already been through this with Eugene. They're deer prints," he insisted. "There are deer all over these woods."

"I don't think so," Stacey said, leaning over to examine the markings more carefully.

"What are you saying?" Eugene yelped.

"I'm saying that these prints don't belong to a deer," Stacey told him. "They're too big."

That was all Eugene needed to hear to keep right on freaking out. "That's because they're the Beast of Baskerville's hoofprints!"

Adam had a different thought. "Maybe they were made by a cow's hoof," he reasoned.

"Are you stupid, or what?" Eugene snapped. "There aren't any cows in these woods!"

"No," Adam shot back, "but there's a cow leg."

"You think Dougie did this, too?" Chris asked.

"Yup," Adam answered, trying to convince himself as much as the others.

"I don't know, Adam," Stacey said. "How would Dougie know we were going to find these prints? It's pitch black out here. And there's no way he's had time to run all around these woods stamping the ground with his cow leg."

"Why don't we just get out of here," Chris suggested, sounding spooked.

"Fine," Adam agreed. "Let's find Eric, Rob, and Jay."

"You go find Eric, Rob, and Jay," Eugene said. "We'll wait in the street."

Stacey and Chris went along with Eugene.

Adam wasn't about to set off on his own.

"Hey, Eric," he called out at the top of his lungs as the four of them headed out of the woods. "Come on out! Forget about Dougie and Travis. And forget about Shauna and Jen, too!"

Adam waited for a response. But the woods were totally quiet. And eerily still.

"Hey, guys!" Adam yelled out again as they hit the street. "Give it up already. There's no point in wasting our whole night playing hide-and-seek with those creeps!"

But there was only one person in the woods playing hide-and-seek. And he was definitely winning.

15

I don't like this," Stacey said as she, Adam, Eugene, and Chris hid behind the water tower across the street from the woods. They were watching and waiting for Dougie and the rest of their friends to resurface.

It had been Adam's idea to hide. He was convinced that the creature who'd grabbed Rob, Eric, and Jay out in the woods was Dougie. He was certain that the three boys were now playing along with Dougie and Travis's disappearing act, too—just like Shauna and Jen. And he was sure that if they waited long enough, Dougie would get bored with his games, and the rest of the gang would show up.

The problem was, they'd been watching and waiting for a good twenty minutes, and there was still no sign of any of the others.

"If this is a joke," Chris said nervously, "it's not very funny."

"Tell me about it," Adam muttered in disgust.

"How much longer are we going to wait for them?" Stacey wanted to know.

"Just another minute," Adam decided, peering around the tower again.

But the woods remained silent—and totally still.

Unfortunately, Eugene did not.

"I hate to tell you this," he said, shining his flashlight on his watch, "but we don't have a lot of minutes left."

"What do you mean?" Chris gulped.

"It's almost eleven thirty," Eugene said.

"Soooooo?" Adam had no idea where Eugene was going with this.

"Soooooo," Eugene huffed, "in another half an hour it's going to be midnight!"

"And what happens then?" Adam asked. "You turn into a pumpkin or something?"

"No!" Eugene snapped. "We all turn into Beast stew!"

Everyone, including Itsy, stared at Eugene.

"It's the Beast's anniversary!" Eugene reminded them as if they were morons. "Don't you get it? He's probably trying to eat his way through this neighborhood before midnight."

"Where did you get that idea?" Adam asked. But he landed on the answer a split second later. "Don't tell me," he said, holding his hand up to Eugene like a stop sign. "Dougie, right?"

Eugene nodded.

"Oh, brother," Adam groaned. "You know what that means, don't you?" He turned to Stacey and Chris.

Stacey and Chris shook their heads.

"It means Dougie's planning to torture us for another half an hour," Adam said, certain it was true.

"Do you really think so?" Chris asked.

"I *know* so," Adam answered. "It's the way Dougie works. He'll do anything for a stupid joke."

"So what are we going to do?" Stacey asked. "Hide out here until twelve?"

"Nah," Adam said. "It's not worth it. If those guys

want to spend the rest of the night acting like jerks, let them. I say we go over to Dee-Dee's tent and grab some food. I'm starving, and Dee-Dee's tent is cram-packed with munchies."

"Good idea," Stacey and Chris both agreed.

But just as they were about to head off, another bloodcurdling scream ripped through the night.

Adam's heart dropped to the pit of his growling stomach as he spun around.

The screams weren't coming from the woods across the street. They were coming from the railroad tracks—from Dee-Dee and Vanessa.

16

As the screaming down by the railroad tracks suddenly stopped, the screaming behind the water tower immediately kicked in.

"There's no point in going to Dee-Dee's tent now!" Eugene cried in a panic. "Because Dee-Dee and Vanessa aren't in it! And you want to know why? Because you're not the only one in this neighborhood looking for munchies!"

Adam was tempted to set Eugene straight, but he didn't want to waste time. "Come on," he said, tearing off down the hill toward the railroad tracks. "How much you want to bet we catch all those guys down here?"

"I thought you said Dougie and the rest of them were hiding in the woods," Stacey reminded him as she followed with Itsy. Behind her, Chris dragged Eugene along.

"They were. But they probably snuck over to Dee-Dee's tent while we were hiding behind the water tower," Adam called back.

"Why would they do that?" Chris wanted to know.

"To get Dee-Dee and Vanessa in on the act, too," Adam answered. "Just in case we went looking for them."

Adam was sure he was right. Especially when he spotted a trail of Bugles leading to the mouth of the sewer pipe.

"Do you see that?" he said, grabbing the flashlight from Eugene's hand and shining it at the ground. "Dee-Dee left us a trail."

"How do you know she didn't drop these before?" Stacey asked, staring down at the Bugles.

"Because they lead into the pipe," he said, directing the light into the foul-smelling tube. One Bugle after the next littered its slimy black bottom. "Dee-Dee didn't go in here before."

"Adam's right," Stacey told Eugene and Chris. "Dee-Dee *didn't* go in here before. So she must have dropped them just now."

"You see, Eugene?" Adam felt smug. "The Beast couldn't have eaten Dee-Dee. Because Dee-Dee's still eating."

"So what do you want to do?" Stacey asked.

"I say we follow these Bugles and nab those guys," Adam answered.

"No way I'm going into that pipe." Eugene freaked at the suggestion.

"Me neither," Chris agreed.

"Fine," Adam shot back. "But when you two are the laughingstock of the neighborhood, I don't want to hear about it. Because I'm going in."

"Itsy and I are going, too," Stacey said. "No way I'm going to be the object of everyone's jokes."

"Then I'm going, too." Chris quickly changed her mind. "I'm not staying out here alone."

"You won't be alone," Eugene said. "You'll be with me."

Chris gave him a skeptical look. "Like I said, I'm going, too."

Thanks to Eugene's "safety in numbers" rule, he had no choice but to follow everyone else.

"Hey, Dougie!" Adam called out as they started through the slimy, foul tube. "We know where you are. Dee-Dee left us a trail."

But as Adam moved deeper and deeper into the pipe, the Bugle trail got harder and harder to follow. In fact, when they rounded the curve and discovered that the pipe split off in opposite directions, the trail disappeared completely.

"Now what?" Stacey asked. She and Itsy were right behind Adam.

"I don't know," Adam admitted, scanning both directions with the flashlight. "It looks like the pipe gets kind of narrow down there," he said, pointing to his left. "So maybe we should go this way."

"Maybe we should go that way!" Eugene cried, pointing back toward the exit.

"I'm with Eugene," Chris agreed. "I mean, who knows where this tunnel will lead," she added nervously. "What if we get lost down here or something?"

Adam was totally frustrated with his friends. "We're

not going to get lost," he insisted. "Look. If we don't find them at the end of *this* tunnel"—he pointed to his right—"we'll turn back, okay?"

"And what if *this* tunnel goes all the way to China?" Eugene snapped. "Some of them do, you know."

"They do not." Adam laughed. "Besides, if we end up in China, you won't have to worry about the Beast anymore, will you?"

"Not unless he's following us." That thought made Eugene shoot up to the front of the line, right behind Adam. It also gave him new incentive to move on. "Just keep going," he told Adam, shoving him forward. "There's got to be another exit in this thing."

There was, too. But it wasn't the kind of exit Adam expected.

"Holy smoke!" he said, startled by the sight. "Look at this. There's a door in this pipe." Adam shone the beam of the flashlight across a huge steel door cut into the side of the pipe.

"Who would put a door in a sewer pipe?" Chris wondered aloud.

"Probably the sewer guys," Adam answered. "I'll bet

there's some kind of utility room behind here. And I'll bet you those creeps are hiding in it."

Adam tried to push the door, but it wouldn't budge.

"Help me out here." He panted with the effort. "This door's really heavy."

Stacey leaned her back against the door next to Adam so she wouldn't have to put Itsy down, while Eugene and Chris squished in between them.

With one good push, the door gave way quickly, sending the four of them toppling to the ground.

Behind them, the steel door immediately clanged shut again.

Adam looked around, suddenly sorry that they hadn't walked straight to China.

The four of them were in a utility room, all right. But it didn't belong to the sewer guys.

17

Adam's heart felt as if it were about to explode as his eyes scanned the terrifying room around him. It looked like some kind of witch's den or a monster's dungeon—Adam couldn't tell which. But one thing was certain—the tools in this room had nothing to do with plumbing.

The walls were lined with bloodstained axes, sickles, and scythes, next to terrible-looking hammerlike things that Adam couldn't begin to identify. But he had the sinking feeling they were used for bone-crunching and skull-smashing.

Above Adam's head, dozens of animal hides dangled

from hooks attached to old, rusted chains th
from the ceiling.

And while Dougie and the rest of their friend. re
nowhere in sight, Adam saw plenty of other kids h ng-
ing around the room. The problem was, they were skeletons. And they were hanging around on poles!

"So this is the sewer guys' room, huh?" Eugene's
nerves were shot. "I don't think so, pal!" he shouted in
Adam's face as he pulled his friend to his feet. "I told
you this wasn't a good idea!" He shook Adam hard.
"But you wouldn't listen to me, would you? Nooooo!
You had to drag us through that stinky poop tube so
we could end up just like those guys!" He pointed to
the skeletons.

"Calm down, Eugene." Adam could barely squeak
out the words past Eugene's tight grip.

"Calm down, Eugene?" Eugene shook Adam harder.
"Do you know where we are?"

"No." Adam shook his head. "Do you?"

"No!" Eugene shouted. "But it doesn't look good!"

"Yeah." Stacey gulped loudly. "And it doesn't look

like we're getting out, either." She and Chris were frantically tugging at the door, with Itsy at their feet.

"Try pushing it instead of pulling," Adam suggested, rushing over to help.

But the door wouldn't open an inch.

"This is just great." Eugene's frenzy was escalating. "We're locked in a sewer room that probably belongs to the Beast! Look at this stuff," he rambled on as he wandered around the room nervously. "I mean, who else would store murdering tools in a sewer?"

"Maybe psycho sewer guys would," Stacey suggested as she continued to work at the door with Adam and Chris.

"I don't think we're that lucky," Eugene told her. "This is definitely the Beast's storage closet. And he'll probably be back any minute to hang up the rest of the bones he's collected tonight!"

Adam wasn't about to admit it, but he was beginning to think the very same thing. "We've got to get out of here!" he cried.

"No kidding!" Chris shot back.

Just then, Eugene let out a bloodcurdling scream.

Adam spun around, expecting to see the Beast—or at least a psycho sewer guy—attacking Eugene. But that wasn't what he saw at all.

"It's just a lizard!" Adam barked nervously as Eugene pointed to the green, creepy creature slithering across the floor.

"It's not just a lizard!" Eugene barked back. "It's Elvira Leeds's husband!"

"What the heck are you talking about?" Adam shrieked, looking down at the floor. But the lizard had scooted out of sight.

"Jimmy Leeds's father, you idiot!" Eugene shouted. "The one the witches turned into a three-headed newt with one eye. That was him!" Eugene insisted. "And he was looking at me all creepy and stuff! This must be Elvira Leeds's witch laboratory or something. I'm telling you, that was her husband!"

Adam wanted to tell Eugene that was impossible—but he couldn't.

"There's got to be another way out of here!" Chris was freaking, too.

"Start looking," Adam instructed the group.

A moment later, Itsy found an escape route.

"Over here," Stacey said as Itsy started to bark at the ceiling. "Look, there's a ladder behind these shelves. And look at the ceiling. There's a trapdoor up there. Good girl, Its." She patted Itsy's head before she scooped her up.

"I wonder what kind of trap is behind it?" Eugene murmured.

"It's the only shot we've got," Adam decided.

"Yeah, well, you go first," Eugene told him.

Adam held his breath as he started to climb the rickety rungs of the ladder. *Please let this thing lead to a way out*, he pleaded silently as he pushed up the square metal door above his head.

The cool night air hit Adam dead in the face. Relief washed over him. "This door leads outside!" he called down to his friends. "Come on!"

Adam was ecstatic . . . until he climbed out into the darkness and saw where he was—the top of Deadman's Hill.

18

O h, no!" Eugene scrambled to take his sneakers off the moment he saw where they were. "We're in deep doo-doo now!"

"If I were you," Adam told Eugene, "I'd keep my feet in those shoes. Because this time, you're not getting mine."

Eugene looked to Stacey.

"You're not getting mine, either," Stacey informed him, standing her ground.

"Forget about it," Chris echoed as Eugene threw her a pleading look.

Itsy barked, too—not that she had any sneakers to worry about.

"I guess it doesn't matter whose shoes I wear anyway." Eugene gulped. "None of us are going to make it down this hill alive. Not with the Beast and his witchy mother, Elvira, lurking about."

"Speaking of witchy mothers," Adam said as he nodded his head toward the Beast Tower, "look who's watching us."

Mrs. Leeds, J.J.'s mother, was sitting in her rocking chair in the lighted attic of her house, peering down at them through the window.

"Maybe we should go knock on her door and see if she'll let us in," Stacey suggested.

"Are you nuts?" Adam shrieked. "I'd rather face the Beast."

"Look." Stacey pushed the point. "If Mrs. Leeds lets us in, we can at least find out if J.J.'s alive. And even if he *is* dead, don't you think we ought to tell his mother? Besides which, we need to call the police!" Stacey was losing it, too.

"And what are we going to tell them?" Adam wanted to know. "That the Beast of Baskerville is having an anniversary party—and nine of our friends were his appetizers?"

"Ten if you count J.J.," Chris pointed out.

"What time is it?" Adam asked Eugene.

Eugene looked at his watch. "It's twelve fifteen," he told Adam, sounding surprised.

"You see?" Adam said, feeling relieved. "It's after twelve. And the four of us are still alive. So the Beast is *not* having an anniversary party."

"Maybe he's just running late," Eugene suggested.

Stacey and Chris exchanged looks. "We need to call the cops," they insisted in unison.

Eugene agreed. "Go see if Mrs. Leeds will let you in," he told Adam.

"And what am I supposed to do if J.J.'s *in* the house?" Adam demanded. "I mean, what am I going to tell Mrs. Leeds then?"

"Tell her the truth," Chris said. "Tell her the rest of our friends are missing. And we think the Beast really is roaming around on her property."

"Or just tell her you need to use her phone," Stacey suggested.

"And what do you think the cops are going to do if I call them with this crazy story?" Adam asked.

"I don't know," Eugene said. "Maybe they'll send out Animal Control or something."

"No, they won't," Adam snapped. "They'll send out a psychiatrist. Because they're going to think I'm out of my mind!"

Adam was beginning to think he *was* out of his mind. "You know what," he told the rest of them. "This is nuts. I don't know what that freaky sewer room was all about, but there's no way the Beast exists. And neither does Elvira. It's just a stupid legend. Besides which, the legend says that Elvira lived in the house and Jimmy lived in the well. Nobody ever said anything about a sewer!"

"Maybe Elvira built the sewer room as some kind of secret workshop," Eugene suggested.

"There were no sewers in the seventeen hundreds!" Adam pointed out.

"Maybe it was some kind of root cellar," Chris chimed

in. "And maybe the sewer company just built around it. They did have root cellars in the seventeen hundreds," she informed Adam. "I read about them in school!"

"So where's the well Elvira supposedly threw Jimmy down, huh?" Adam wanted to know.

Just then, Itsy started to sniff at the ground. A moment later she took off past the house.

"It-sy!" Stacey shrieked. "Get back here!"

Itsy kept going.

"I've got to go get her!" Stacey cried.

"Why?" Eugene huffed. "Won't she go home by herself?"

"No!" Stacey said. "She never goes out alone."

"Aw, man," Eugene sighed. "This just isn't happening."

"Come on, you guys," Stacey begged. "You've got to go with me."

At Stacey's insistence, they all took off after Itsy. As they did, Mrs. Leeds got up from her chair and moved closer to the window.

"Something tells me we're not going to have to call the cops," Adam said, gesturing upward. "Because J.J.'s mom is going to do it for us."

In the distance, Itsy started to bark loudly.

As the four of them rounded the house, they saw Itsy scratching at the door of a dilapidated old barn. The door was slightly ajar, and a dim yellow light showed through the crack.

"Get over here, Itsy!" Stacey demanded.

But Itsy stayed put.

"Shut her up already, before she attracts the Beast!" Eugene cried.

As Stacey rushed to the barn, Itsy managed to push her way past the door. Before Stacey could grab her, Itsy had disappeared inside.

"What the heck is she doing?" Adam wondered as he and Stacey pulled open the door and followed Itsy into the barn.

His stomach clenched as he got his answer. Itsy was leading them to a huge stone well.

19

Adam could barely catch his breath. A round stone structure rose from the center of the barn. Now there was no way for Adam to convince himself that the legend of Jimmy Leeds was just a story—not when he was facing the one thing he had believed never existed.

"Oh, my gosh!" Stacey gasped, echoing Adam's thoughts. "This is the well! The one Elvira Leeds threw Jimmy down!"

Adam had never seen a well so big and so creepy.

The circular wall rising out of the ground stood a good four feet high and created a shaft nearly twenty feet in diameter. Instead of a bucket, a huge wooden platform was suspended above the opening. The platform looked like a swing dangling from the end of a thick, heavy rope. The rope was wrapped around a huge steel bar that arched above the well's walls. The free end of the rope was anchored to a big metal crank that stood by the side of the well.

Next to the crank, Itsy was jumping up and down, as though she were trying to figure out how to turn it.

"Get away from there, Its!" Adam shouted at the dog.

Just then, Eugene and Chris came flying into the barn behind them.

The moment Eugene saw the well, he stopped dead in his tracks.

"Holy smokes!" Chris shrieked. "Is that what I think it is?"

Stacey nodded, wide-eyed.

Eugene glared at Adam. "I thought you said there was no well." His mouth kept going. "I mean, 'How the heck do you hide a three-thousand-pound tunnel that's made out of stone?'" he mimicked Adam. "Does this answer your question?" he yelled.

Adam suddenly felt about as big as Itsy. "Look," he

told Eugene, "you were right about the well, okay? But that doesn't mean the rest of the story is true. I mean, think about it," he said, trying to convince himself as much as Eugene. "If the Beast really was still living down in this well, wouldn't J.J. and his mom have seen him already?"

"Maybe they have," Eugene replied. "Maybe they're friends with him."

"Come on, Eugene," Adam coaxed. "That doesn't make any sense."

"Neither does the sewer room," Eugene said. "But it's down there, isn't it?"

"Uh, guys," Chris gulped nervously. "Could we just catch the dog and get out of here—in case you-know-who really is in this well?"

"Good idea," Stacey agreed. She took a step toward the crank to grab Itsy. Suddenly Itsy ran forward. Then, before Stacey could get hold of her, the little dog jumped onto the wall of the well.

"Itsy, get down!" Stacey shrieked, rushing to the ledge. But Itsy dove onto the platform, which was suspended in midair.

"Do something, Adam!" Stacey cried in a panic. "Help!"

Adam ran for the wall, but the platform and Itsy had started to drop.

"Grab the crank!" Adam shouted at Eugene as he tried to reach over the wall to catch hold of the rope.

"What crank?" Eugene cried back.

"That crank!" Adam shouted again. "Hang on, Itsy!" he called down to the dog. He could barely see her anymore. But a strange, eerie light glowing at the bottom of the well told Adam that the drop was a good fifty feet. Itsy was disappearing quickly.

By the time Eugene finally managed to reel up the platform, it was empty.

"Oh, no," Chris gasped. "Itsy's gone!"

Adam's heart dropped faster than Itsy had. Maybe the Beast really was in the well. Maybe he just ate Itsy!

Stacey started to freak. "I want my dog!" she cried.

Just then, a little yip drifted up from the pit below.

"She's okay!" Chris exclaimed. "Itsy's okay!"

"We've got to get her out of there," Stacey told Adam.

Adam was thinking the very same thing. "Drop

that platform," he told Eugene. "Maybe we can get Itsy to climb back on. Then we can reel her back up."

Eugene did as Adam instructed. But no matter how hard the four of them begged, Itsy refused to step onto the board.

"Now what are we going to do?" Adam wondered aloud.

"We have to go down there and get her," Stacey insisted. "It's the only way to get her out."

"Is she out of her mind?" Eugene shot Adam a look. "No way I'm going down into that well! I hate that dog anyway!"

Chris refused to go, too—even though she assured Stacey that she "*loooooved* Itsy." She just didn't love Itsy enough to risk her life for her.

"I'm going down there," Stacey told her friends, "with or without you guys."

Adam knew there was no way he'd be able to talk Stacey out of it. He also knew there was no way he'd ever be able to live with himself if something terrible happened to her. So he decided he had to go with her.

"I can't believe you're doing this over a yippy dog,"

Eugene told Adam as he and Stacey climbed onto the wall of the well.

"Just shut up and listen to me, Eugene," Adam said. "When Stacey and I get onto the platform, you and Chris hold on to that crank so you can control the speed of our drop, you got me?"

Eugene nodded.

"Don't let us drop real fast," Stacey pleaded.

"We won't," Chris assured her.

"Yeah," Adam said. "And the second we grab Itsy, crank us back up as fast as you can."

Adam took hold of the rope and pulled the platform over to the ledge of the well. Then he positioned the platform on top of the wall. As Adam sat down on the board, he let his legs dangle over the side and into the well.

A moment later, Stacey did the same. There was just enough room for the both of them.

"Just hang on to the rope, and don't look down," Adam instructed Stacey.

Stacey nodded.

"Are you guys ready?" he asked Eugene and Chris.

"Ready as we'll ever be," Eugene gulped.

Adam and Stacey pushed off.

The platform swung out to the center of the well, dropping several feet quickly.

Adam's stomach did the same. *"Whoooooaaaaaa!"* He let out a scream.

"Don't worry, buddy!" Eugene cried out. "We've got you!"

A moment later, their descent into the cold, dank, dark, smelly pit became steadier.

Adam heaved a sigh of relief. "You okay?" he asked Stacey.

"Yeah," Stacey answered, hanging on for dear life.

"Is everything all right down there?" Chris called into the pit.

"So far, so good," Adam called back up.

But "so far" wasn't even halfway. And "so good" was about to turn into something far worse than Adam—or even Eugene—ever could have imagined.

20

As Adam and Stacey continued to drop into the pit, he noticed that the walls of the well were beginning to change. The massive gray stones weren't covered with furry green moss and black oozing slime anymore. They were covered with wallpaper!

Adam blinked hard. He was sure he was imagining things. But Stacey saw the shiny gold wallpaper, too.

"Do you see what I see?" she shrieked.

Adam was too terrified to speak; he just nodded.

Suddenly, it looked as if they were dropping into the foyer of a nineteenth-century home, not into the pit of a filthy old well.

Below them, Adam could see two antique torch lamps burning. The lamps stood on opposite sides of a crushed velvet sofa that sat in the center of the well. A marble coffee table stood in front of that. And instead of hitting rock bottom, Adam and Stacey actually landed on a plush carpet.

"Somebody is living down here!" Stacey cried the moment they touched down.

Adam saw with surprise that the circular wall wasn't solid anymore. In fact, there were three doorways cut into the stone.

Luckily, the doors were closed and Itsy hadn't figured out a way to open them yet, although she was scratching against one of them, desperately trying.

"Just grab that dog and let's get out of here!" Adam ordered.

As Stacey ran for Itsy, Adam noticed two paintings hanging on the walls on either side of the door where Itsy was scratching. The painting to the left of the door was a portrait of an evil-looking woman dressed in black. Adam couldn't see her face clearly because there was a veil painted over it. Under the portrait was a plaque that read MOTHER.

To the right of the door was a much smaller painting. Adam had to take a few steps forward before he could make out what it was.

Suddenly, the blood in his veins ran cold. It was a portrait of "Father"—but the image in the frame wasn't human. "Father" was a three-headed newt with only one eye!

Now Adam knew that the somebody living down in the well really was Jimmy Leeds! Because the portraits were definitely paintings of his parents.

"Come on, Stace!" Adam cried. "We've got to get out of here!"

Stacey struggled with Itsy, who had to be taken by force. The moment the dog was safely secured in Stacey's arms, and Stacey and Adam were seated back on the platform, Adam tugged on the rope.

"Start cranking, you guys!" he screamed upward.

Their seat didn't budge.

"Eu-gene!" Adam called out again. "Get us out of here!"

Adam held tight. But still they didn't move.

"Hey, guys!" Stacey yelled, too. "What the heck are you doing up there?"

There was no answer.

"Maybe they don't hear us," Adam suggested nervously, as Stacey turned pale. He tugged on the rope again, hard, hoping that would attract Eugene's attention.

No response.

Adam started to sweat.

"What are we going to do now?" Stacey yelped.

There was only one answer. "We're going to have to climb up these ropes," Adam said.

"Climb the ropes?" Stacey shrieked. "I can't do that."

"Don't worry," Adam told her. "I'll carry Itsy. I'm really good at scaling a rope."

"The problem's not Itsy," Stacey explained. "The problem is the rope."

"What do you mean?" Adam asked.

"I mean, I can't climb it!" Stacey shouted. "I failed all that stuff in gym class. I can't do the balance beam. And I can't climb a rope even when there are knots tied in it."

"You're kidding me, right?" Adam said hopefully.

Stacey shook her head.

"Then you and Itsy are going to have to wait here while I climb up," Adam decided quickly.

"You can't leave Itsy and me down here alone," Stacey said.

Adam didn't want to. But he didn't have a choice. "Look," he said. "If I don't climb up, we may never get out. I promise I'll climb real fast. And the minute I get to the top, I'll crank you up, too."

Stacey seemed to realize there was no other way. "Just hurry," she told Adam as he reached for the rope.

Adam wrapped his hands around the thick, heavy line. Then he gripped the rope with his feet and started to move his body upward.

By the time he was thirty feet up, Adam's arms started to ache. He was beginning to worry that he wouldn't make it all the way to the top. "Hey, Eugene!" he called out again. "Start cranking, will you?"

Still there was no answer.

This time, Adam knew he was close enough to the

mouth of the well for Eugene to hear him. Something had to be wrong.

With all the strength he could muster, Adam pulled himself upward.

Finally, he hauled himself over the wall.

Eugene and Chris were nowhere in sight.

"Hey, guys?" Adam swallowed hard as his eyes scanned the barn. "Where are you?"

The barn was perfectly still.

No way those guys took off without us, Adam thought in a panic. Then he screamed into the well. "Stacey, can you hear me?"

"Yeah." Stacey's voice echoed loud and clear.

"Get ready," Adam called. "I'll reel you up."

"Okay," Stacey called back.

Adam grabbed hold of the crank. But his arms were aching so badly from his long climb, he could barely get it to budge. There was no way he'd be able to lift Stacey and Itsy up all by himself.

"Hurry up!" Stacey cried. "I think I hear somebody moving around down here!"

Adam's adrenaline started to pump. But still he

could manage to lift Stacey only three or four feet off the ground before he had to let her drop again.

"What are you doing?" Stacey shrieked.

"Just hang on, Stace," Adam shouted down. "I'll get you up in a minute."

Adam knew he wasn't going to be able to keep that promise without help. He ran for the door, hoping to spot Eugene and Chris.

But there wasn't a soul to be seen.

Adam took off for the hill. But Deadman's Hill was dead as could be.

Do something! Adam ordered himself as he rushed back toward the barn. The thought of Stacey alone in that well had him terrified. What if something happened to her?

Just then, Adam remembered J.J.'s mom. He had to ask her for help now. There was no other way.

"Mrs. Leeds!" Adam cried up to the Beast Tower. But the Beast Tower was dead as the hill. The lights were out and the rocking chair was empty. He was about to run for the house and pound on the door when he heard Stacey scream.

"Hang on, Stacey!" Adam yelled as he ran for the barn instead. "I'm coming!"

By the time Adam reached the stone wall, the screaming had stopped.

"Stacey?" he called into the well in a panic. "What's going on down there? Are you okay?"

A moment later, Adam got a reply. But it wasn't from Stacey.

21

I'll tell you what's going on down here, you moron!" another voice boomed from the depths of the well. "The Beast of Baskerville is throwing a little party. And your stupid friend Stacey just got herself invited, right along with that mangy-looking yippy dog I can't stand."

Adam's heart twisted into one giant knot. He was so terrified, he could barely breathe, much less speak. And he was so startled by the sound of the voice that it took him a full minute to realize he recognized it.

"Am I talking to myself?" the voice in the pit snapped viciously. "Or do you hear me up there?"

"Calm down, J.J.," Adam managed to say. "I hear you, okay?"

"Calm down?" J.J. growled. "It's twelve thirty-eight already," he told Adam. "The Beast's party is going to be over in twenty-two minutes."

That's one A.M., Adam thought. *Maybe Eugene was right. Maybe the Beast really is running late.* "What are you doing down there?" he called out to J.J.

"I'm the party coordinator, you shmoe," J.J. shot back. "What do you think I'm doing down here?"

Even under the worst circumstances, J.J. was still a booger ball.

"I mean did the Beast drag you down there?" Adam wanted to know. "Or did you climb down yourself?"

"I got tossed down," J.J. answered. "But the rest of these clowns got dragged. Except for Stacey, of course; she came down by herself. And Eugene got carried."

"Eugene's down there, too?" Adam gasped.

"No," J.J. said sarcastically, "I'm lying."

"When did you see Eugene?" Adam asked.

"A few minutes ago," J.J. answered. "The Beast carried him here through one of the sewer pipes that's connected to this stinking rat hole. And he was dragging Chris behind him by the ankle."

"Were they alive?" Adam was almost afraid to ask.

"What am I, a medical examiner?" J.J. snapped. "Chris was squiggling a lot," he told Adam. "But Eugene was limp."

"Didn't you try to help them?" Adam asked.

"No, I didn't try to help them," J.J. snarled back. "I've been kind of busy tonight trying to save my own butt! Now are you going to come down here and help me out of this jam, or what?"

"Seems to me that if the Beast is down there, you ought to come up here!" Adam told the little genius.

For a moment there was silence. Then J.J. suddenly changed his tune. "I just figured if you came down here, we could try to save everyone else, too."

"Not in twenty minutes, we can't," Adam cried. "We have to get your mom! She has to call the police!"

"Nooooooooo!" J.J.'s voice dropped twelve angry octaves before it rose from the well. "Don't you dare get my mom!"

"Why not?" Adam was startled.

"Because she won't believe you," J.J. said, sounding a little more composed. "She'll think you're making it up. Then everyone will be doomed."

"Then you tell her," Adam insisted. "She'll listen to you, won't she?"

"Not in this lifetime," J.J. grumbled.

"Then I'm going to get her," Adam said. "It's the only chance we've got."

"No, you're not!" J.J.'s voice dropped deeper than the well again. "I'll tell her, okay?"

"Fine," Adam agreed.

"Just come down and get me," J.J. demanded again.

"I'm not going to come down and get you," Adam said. "Then we'll both be stuck, you jerk. Climb up the rope."

"I don't want to climb," J.J. told him.

"Then get onto that platform and I'll try to reel you up." Adam was disgusted.

"Make it fast," J.J. ordered.

As soon as Adam felt a tug on the rope, he started to crank. This time, it wasn't Adam's arms that gave out before he could lift J.J. to safety. It was the tension in the rope. Suddenly, it felt as if J.J. had slipped off the platform.

What the heck is he doing? Adam was getting ticked off. "Hey, J.J.!" he shouted into the pit. "You've got to hang on to the rope."

There was no answer.

"J.J.?" Adam called out again, leaning over the wall of the well. "Are you okay?"

There was still no response.

Adam's heart started to pound.

Maybe J.J. didn't slip off the platform, he thought. *Maybe somebody pulled him off!*

As Adam's eyes scanned the pit, he caught sight of something purple and shiny just two feet below him. It was the tip of J.J.'s "Birthday Boy" elephant hat. The problem was, the hat was resting between two twisted goat horns on the top of a huge hairy head!

The Beast was climbing out of the well!

"Surprise!" The creature clinging to the wall tilted his massive head upward and glared at Adam with fiery red eyes.

Adam turned to run. But before he had taken even

one step, the cloven-hoofed creature leaped over the wall and grabbed Adam by the back of his neck.

"It's party time, pal!" The Beast in the hat laughed maniacally. "And you're the last guest of honor!"

22

Let me go!" Adam screamed as the Beast picked him up and threw him over his hairy shoulder.

"As soon as the party's over," the Beast growled, carrying Adam to the wall of the well.

Adam was sure the Beast was going to pitch him over the side of the well, just as Elvira had pitched little Jimmy so many years ago. But Adam knew there was no way he would survive the fifty-foot drop.

"Don't drop me!" he cried, kicking the Beast's hairy gut and punching his furry back furiously.

"Then shut up!" the Beast commanded. "Because if you wake my mom, I swear I'll eat your heart out!"

"Your mom?" Adam gulped.

"Yeah," the Beast said, "my mom. She's not invited to this party. And if you don't stop kicking and punching me, I'll crush your bones. I can do that, you know."

Adam felt the grip around his body tighten like a vise. He was painfully aware that bone-crunching was a skill the Beast had mastered.

"I'll stop! I'll stop!" Adam gasped with the last bit of air the Beast squeezed from his chest.

"Good move," the Beast said as Adam stopped fighting.

"So where *is* your mom?" Adam asked as the Beast leaped onto the wall of the well.

"In the house," he answered, "sleeping."

"Your mom lives in the house?" Adam was astounded.

"No," the Beast cracked. "She lives on the moon. Of course she lives in the house." He grabbed the rope and swung them both out to the center of the well.

Adam let out a scream.

"Keep it up," the Beast said, "and I'll rip out your lungs with my hands."

Adam was pretty sure that ripping out lungs was a skill the Beast had mastered as well. So he shut up.

As they slid down the rope, Adam prayed there'd be no ripping out of organs at all. If the Beast was going to eat him, Adam hoped it would be in one bite. At least that way it would be quick.

The moment they hit the bottom, the Beast set Adam down on his feet. "My back is killing me," he complained.

Adam was about to run for one of the doors in hope of escaping, but the Beast immediately pulled his feet out from under him. Adam fell flat on his back.

"This is much easier," the Beast said as he grabbed Adam's ankles and started dragging him across the carpet.

Easier for who? Adam thought.

"Although," the Beast continued, "I've got to tell you that dragging Dee-Dee around was no picnic."

"Dee-Dee's down here, too?" Adam asked.

"Everybody's down here," the Beast said. "Tent night has moved underground." He laughed.

How did the Beast know it was tent night?

"So, how do you like my humble abode?" the Beast asked Adam.

"It's great," Adam answered. "I really like it a lot."

"Liar," the Beast growled. Then he pulled Adam through one of the doors. "This place stinks," he said, dragging Adam down what looked like another sewer pipe. "You try living in a well for two hundred and twenty-six years, *then* tell me how much you like it."

Adam gulped. This was not a happy Beast. "So why don't you move out?" he asked hesitantly.

"Where to?" the Beast said. "Your house?"

No way, Jose! Adam thought. But he kept his mouth shut. Still, the Beast gave him a look.

"I didn't think so," the Beast snorted.

"So why don't you live in the house with your mom?" Adam asked.

"Because she's a witch," the Beast snapped. "All she does is nag, nag, nag, nag! 'Jimmy, get this.'" He mimicked his mother's voice. "'Jimmy, get that. Where are those slug brains you were supposed to dig up for me, Jimmy? And what about those lizard bellies? When are you going to get those? You know I can't do my

148

spells without them. And don't forget about the Kenny gizzards and the Mary meat that I need.'" The Beast shook his head in disgust. "Nothing I ever do for that woman is enough."

"What's 'Kenny gizzards' and 'Mary meat'?" Adam asked nervously. He was pretty clear on the slug brains and the lizard bellies.

"What's it sound like, you moron?" the Beast huffed. "It's gizzards from Kennys and chopped meat from Marys. It's the only way to put a spell on people named Kenny and Mary. They were our neighbors once," he informed Adam. "Before my mom turned them into horny-backed toads."

"Your mom doesn't sound very nice," Adam said hesitantly.

"No kidding," the Beast said. "I told you, she's a witch!"

"And what about your dad?" Adam asked. "What's he like?"

"My dad's okay," the Beast answered. "But he's a newt. So it's not like we can do anything fun together. You know what I mean?"

A newt for a dad? No. Adam didn't know what he meant. But he nodded anyway. "That's too bad," he said, trying to sound sympathetic.

"Yeah," the Beast agreed. "My dad can't play baseball with me or anything. And I don't have any friends in the neighborhood to play with, either."

What a surprise! Adam thought. "I guess it's hard to have any friends when you eat them," he couldn't resist saying.

"I don't eat anybody," the Beast said.

"You don't?" Adam swallowed hard.

"No. That legend stuff is a bunch of baloney. I'm actually a nice guy," the Beast insisted. "But no one wants to believe it."

Given that Adam was being dragged by his ankles through sewerlike tunnels at the bottom of a well, he could understand how the nice-guy image wasn't quite getting across. But he wasn't about to point that out to the Beast. "So you're not going to eat me?" he asked.

"No," the Beast answered. "But if you screw up my party, I'll bash in your head."

This was hardly the reassurance Adam was hoping

to hear. "Don't worry," he said. "I won't screw up your party. I promise."

"Yeah?" the Beast challenged. "Well, you've got thirteen minutes and fifty-seven seconds to live up to that promise. Otherwise, you're a pile of Adam gizzards, you got me?"

"Loud and clear," Adam said.

"Good." The Beast smiled as he dragged Adam through another series of pipes.

"So what kind of party is this?" Adam asked.

"A birthday party," the Beast said. "The one you were trying to weasel out of."

23

"You're dragging me to J.J.'s birthday party?" Adam asked.

"I *am* J.J., you idiot," the Beast snapped.

Either the Beast was a real "genius" too, or he was messing with Adam's head.

"How can you be J.J.?" Adam asked. "J.J.'s not a . . ." Adam was about to say "beast," but he quickly changed his mind.

"J.J.'s not a what?" the Beast growled.

"He's not a . . . big guy like you," Adam stumbled.

"Yeah, I know," the Beast said. "He's a booger boy, right?"

Adam wasn't about to say yes. Maybe Eugene was right. Maybe J.J. and his mom really were friends with the Beast. And maybe if he said the wrong thing, the Beast *would* bash his head in. "No," Adam lied. "He's a genius."

The Beast laughed. "You got that right," he said.

"So, if you're J.J.," Adam asked, "what's your first name?" Adam was sure the Beast wouldn't know the right answer to this one. But he did.

"The *J*s are my name," the Beast said quickly, mimicking J.J.

Holy smokes! Adam thought. *This is J.J.!*

"You thought you had me there, didn't you?" the Beast sneered. "But guess what? The *J*s really are just initials. You want to know what they stand for?" he asked.

Adam nodded, swallowing hard.

"James Joseph Leeds," the Beast informed him. "But you can call me Jimmy."

"How can that be?" Adam wondered aloud. "J.J.'s only thirteen years old."

"I only *look* thirteen," the Beast explained, still

sounding like J.J. "And that's just during the day. It was all part of the curse the other witches put on my mom."

"I thought they turned you into a beast before you were born," Adam said.

"They did," the Beast replied. "But I'm not a beast all the time."

Could have fooled me, Adam thought. *Horns or no horns.*

"Look," the Beast said impatiently, "here's how it works. I only turn into the Beast at the hour of my birth, which is ten fifty-eight P.M. Then I stay that way until sunrise, at which point I turn human again. It's kind of like being a werewolf, only worse. Because I have to transform every night, with or without a full moon."

"Then how come you're not like two hundred years old during the day?" Adam asked.

"Because thirteen witches cursed me," the Beast said. "So when I'm human, I'm eternally stuck at that number. Which really stinks," he told Adam. "I can never grow up and get rid of my mom. Unless, of course, I break the curse."

"And how do you do that?" Adam asked.

"By throwing a birthday party," the Beast replied.

Adam couldn't believe his ears. "You mean to tell me that all you have to do to stop being the Beast is throw a birthday party?"

"Yeah," he said. "And I have to get thirteen humans to sing 'Happy Birthday' to me while I am the Beast. And they have to do it before the thirteenth hour. Then, when I blow out my thirteen candles, the curse will be broken. And I'll get to live a normal life."

Suddenly, Adam felt sorry for the Beast. He wasn't trying to hurt anyone. He was just trying to have a birthday party!

"But as you can see," the Beast continued, "it's not very easy for me to make friends. Plus, I only get a shot at this birthday party stuff every thirteenth year after the moon is full on the thirteenth day of the month before my birth, thanks to the rules of the witch club my mother belonged to," he complained to Adam. "Do you have any idea how hard it is to keep track of this stuff?"

"I can imagine," Adam said, trying to sound sympathetic.

"No, you can't!" the Beast roared, sounding anything but comforted.

"Good thing you're a genius," Adam said, trying to warm him back up again.

"Ain't that the truth." The Beast's tone softened a bit. "Still, it's not easy. You should have seen the last party I had. It was a total disaster."

"What happened?" Adam asked.

"My mom put the kibosh on it," the Beast said.

"What did she do?" Adam wanted to know.

"She killed every kid in Baskerville. And trust me when I tell you," the Beast added as he dragged Adam through the doors of what looked like an underground dining room. "If she finds out about this one, she'll definitely do it again."

24

As the Beast hauled Adam into the "party" room, Adam looked around at the rest of the "guests." While he was grateful to see that all his friends were present and accounted for, he also saw that none of them looked very happy. In fact, they looked tortured. Except for Eugene—he was out cold in the corner.

"Eugene!" Adam gasped at the sight.

"Don't worry," the Beast assured him. "He's not dead. He got so scared he passed out. That's all."

Adam heaved a sigh of relief as he scanned the rest of his friends.

Every one of them was wearing a party hat. But it

was quite clear that no one was in a partying mood. Especially since they were all strapped to their chairs and gagged with their elephant napkins, including Itsy, who was tied to the seat next to Stacey.

In front of the guests was a huge dining room table covered with a purple tablecloth. On top of the table were thirteen paper elephant plates, cups, and forks. J.J. must have scooped up the elephant cake from the street—it was pieced back together, covered with dirt, and sitting in the center of the table. Thirteen purple candles were crammed into it.

Hanging on the wall was a giant pin the tail on Dee-Dee game—a game inspired by Dee-Dee herself.

"You like that?" the Beast asked Adam, pointing out the donkeyed Dee-Dee. "I drew it myself."

"It's great," Adam said, remembering the Beast's bone-crunching, head-smashing skills. "Looks just like her."

The Beast laughed.

"So let me ask you something," Adam said. "What's with all this elephant stuff?" He couldn't resist asking.

"Nothing," the Beast answered. "I just like elephants, that's all."

"Oh," Adam said. *You really are a genius, aren't you?*

"Don't you like elephants?" The Beast's question interrupted Adam's thoughts.

"Love them," Adam answered. Then his thoughts turned back to Elvira and the Beast's saying she would kill every kid in Baskerville if she caught them having a party—elephants or not. "So listen," he told the Beast. "Don't you think we ought to start singing or something? We're running out of time."

"Good idea," the Beast agreed, pulling Adam to his feet. "I don't have to strap you to a chair or anything, do I?"

Adam shook his head. "Trust me," he said. "I'm dying to sing. But you better ungag the rest of these guys. Otherwise they won't be able to sing 'Happy Birthday.'"

"You're right," the Beast decided. He pulled the gag from Dougie's mouth first.

"*Aaaaaaaaaagggggghhhhh!*" Dougie wailed like a storm.

The Beast quickly crammed the gag back in. "He's been doing that all night," he told Adam. "Ever since I pulled him out of the sewer pipe."

Just then, Adam had a horrible thought. *If the Beast really did pull Dougie out of the sewer, maybe that really was blood in the street!* He quickly looked at Shauna and Jen. Their heads were still on, but it was Shauna's feet he was worried about. He leaned over to look under the table.

The Beast noticed. "What's the matter?"

"Nothing," Adam lied, searching for a shoeless foot.

"You're looking for Shauna's feet, aren't you?" the Beast asked.

Adam nodded.

"Don't worry," he said. "They're still there. I just thought that leaving the sneaker and the hair clip in a puddle of blood would be a nice touch."

"That was really blood?" Adam's stomach lurched.

"No," the Beast said. "It was tomato juice—from Dougie's cow leg. I was going to save it for the cake because I didn't have time to buy any soda," he told Adam. "But I dumped it in the street instead."

Stacey was looking at Adam like he was nuts.

"Didn't you tell these guys who you are?" Adam asked the Beast.

"No," he said. "Nobody asked."

Just then, Eugene came to. The moment he opened his eyes, he started to scream.

"Give me that napkin!" Adam cried, terrified that Eugene's voice was going to travel right through the sewer and up to Elvira. The Beast handed one over. Adam crammed it into Eugene's mouth. "Shut up, you jerk!" he told Eugene. "You're going to get us all killed!"

Everyone in the room glared at Adam.

"Listen to me, guys," he started to explain. "The Beast is really J.J.—James Joseph Leeds," he told them. "And J.J.'s mom is really Elvira. And she really was cursed by a bunch of witches—thirteen to be exact. But J.J. doesn't like being the Beast. And he's not the Beast all the time. He only turns into the Beast at ten fifty-eight P.M., right?"

The Beast nodded as Adam continued.

"J.J. wants to be normal—or at least as normal as J.J. can be," Adam clarified. "And the only way he can do that is by breaking the curse. And the only way he can do *that* is if thirteen human kids sing him 'Happy Birthday' tonight before the thirteenth hour. You got it?"

Everyone was still looking at Adam as if he were nuts.

"So when I pull your gags out, everyone start singing really fast," he instructed. "And no screaming," he ordered. "Otherwise, we'll be asking for trouble." He turned to the Beast. "Light those candles, J.J.," he said, "and let's get this show on the road."

The Beast struck a match as Adam ran around the room pulling out gags. Everyone was following his instructions, including Eugene and Dougie.

"Ready?" he asked the group as he looked down at Eugene's watch. It was twelve fifty-six and thirty-three seconds. They only had three minutes and twenty-seven seconds to go. It was then that Adam realized he'd forgotten to ask the Beast one very important question. *What happens to us if he doesn't blow these candles out by the thirteenth hour?*

Adam wasn't about to wait and see. "Sing!" he commanded the group. "Fast!"

"Happy birthday to you. Happy birthday to you. Happy birthday dear . . ." Everyone looked to the Beast.

"Jimmy," he said.

"Jimmy," they sang. "Happy birthday to you."

The Beast sucked in a deep breath. He was ready to blow, with three minutes and twenty-three seconds to spare. But the air from his gut never hit the candles.

Just then, his witchy mother, Elvira, flew into the room and rammed him with her broomstick.

The party was over.

25

W hat did I tell you about birthday parties?" Elvira Leeds bellowed at the Beast. "Birthday parties are for other people! Not for you!" She smacked the Beast in the head with the bristles of her broom.

Everyone was shocked into silence as Elvira went on her rampage.

The Beast started to shake like a scared little kid. "Sorry, Mom," he said, in the voice of a mouse.

"Sorry's not good enough," the old woman croaked. "What are you trying to do—get me killed?"

The Beast shook his head.

"Bull gizzards," Elvira shot back. "You know exactly what will happen to me if you blow out these candles!"

The Beast might have known, but Adam certainly didn't. *Uh-oh,* Adam thought. *Something tells me this is the part of the story J.J. left out.*

"Now I'm going to have to spend the rest of the night killing all these kids," she huffed.

With that news flash, everyone in the room started to scream, including Adam.

"Shut your traps," Elvira shouted at the group. She pointed her twisted finger at Dougie, who was screaming the loudest. Then she uttered a few magic words that sounded like "Ah-gul-de-bah-gul-de-tongue."

Immediately, Dougie's tongue started to grow. It twisted out of his mouth like a snake being charmed from its basket. Then it tied itself into six knots, before the knotted part flopped to the floor.

Adam couldn't believe his eyes.

"Who's next?" Elvira cackled maliciously.

The room quickly fell silent.

"That's better," Elvira sighed. Then she turned her

attention back to J.J. and screamed like a banshee. "I can't go through this every time you get a lucky thirteen!" she shouted. "There's only so much a mother can take!"

As Elvira kept ranting, Adam inched his way over to Eugene to look down at his watch.

One minute and counting.

"We've got to get Elvira away from J.J.," Adam whispered to Eugene without moving his lips, "so that J.J. can blow out those candles. Otherwise we're dead."

Eugene shook his head no.

"You have to help me, Eugene," Adam said. "Everyone else is tied up."

"Are you nuts?" Eugene barely made a sound. "If we even try to move, she's liable to tie our *legs* into knots."

"And if we don't make a move, she'll kill us!" Adam told him.

Forty-five seconds and counting.

"What do you want me to do?" Eugene asked.

"I want you to create a diversion," Adam said.

"A what?" Eugene's terrified face looked confused.

"A diversion," Adam repeated. "As soon as I move to

the other side of the table, I want you to start scream-ing. That way, when Elvira turns to look at you, I can ram her from behind."

"Forget it," Eugene said. "There's no way you're going to be able to ram her before she starts saying that ah-gul-de-bah-gul-de stuff."

"That's why *you* have to do it," Adam urged. "So you can jump out of the way the moment she lifts her finger."

Twenty-three seconds and counting.

"You have to, Eugene," Adam insisted.

"If my tongue grows," Eugene threatened, "I swear I'm going to tie it into my own knot—right around your throat!"

"Don't worry." Adam tried to sound brave. "We can do this."

As Adam inched his way back around the table, Elvira was still yelling.

"You're not a genius, J.J.," she shouted at the Beast. "You're an imbecile! A stinking, hairy imbecile!"

With less than ten seconds to spare, Adam mouthed the word "go" to Eugene.

Eugene started to wail.

Elvira spun toward the sound. As she did, Adam lunged forward.

"Blow!" Adam screamed at the Beast before he tackled Elvira from behind.

The Beast filled his hairy gut with air, then blew it out like a gale wind. This time, he actually hit the cake.

One second before the thirteenth hour, the thirteen candles went out.

"I did it!" the Beast exclaimed. "I blew out the candles!"

"You did it, all right!" Elvira shrieked. Then she turned her twisted finger at Adam and sent him flying up to the ceiling. "It's dead time for you, buster!" she told him.

Adam's back hit the ceiling hard. He was stuck to the roof of the room like a bug stuck to a fly strip!

Below him, Eugene was covering his mouth with his hands.

"Out come your innards, honey!" Elvira screeched, pointing up at Adam. "And off come your limbs!"

Adam was close to passing out when he noticed that someone else's limbs were falling off instead.

168

Holy smokes! he thought as he watched Elvira's arms drop from her body and land on the floor. A moment later, her legs gave way, too.

The curse really was broken!

Elvira Leeds was falling to pieces. And the Beast was turning back into a boy.

26

Within seconds, Elvira Leeds was nothing but a pile of body parts. And Jimmy Leeds was jumping up and down for joy.

Adam was down from the ceiling. Dougie's tongue was back in his mouth.

"You saved me!" Jimmy told Adam. "You actually saved me!"

Adam smiled. While Jimmy Leeds still looked just like J.J., somehow there was something less beastly about him.

"So how about saving the rest of us, uh . . . Jimmy?" Dee-Dee blurted.

"You got it," Jimmy said. He started to untie his thirteen honored guests. "You know," he told them, "you guys don't have to call me Jimmy. You can call me J.J. if you want. Or you can call me J. You can even call me Joseph. But don't ever call me the Beast again."

"Don't worry," Stacey said as Jimmy untied her. "We won't."

"So, J.J." Eugene swallowed hard. "What are you going to do now? I mean, now that you killed your mother?"

"I didn't *kill* my mother," Jimmy explained. "She just disappeared with the curse. That's why she never wanted me to have a birthday party. Because once I broke the curse of her coven, she was a goner. It's one of those witch rules. Besides," he told them, "I still have my dad."

"Yeah, but isn't he a newt?" Eugene asked.

"Not anymore," Jimmy informed them. "According to witch law, my dad had to turn back to normal, too. Finally we'll get to do something together besides catching bugs."

"Uhh . . . that's great," Eric said.

"So where will you live?" Stacey wanted to know.

"Not in this sewer," Jimmy told her. "That's for sure. But you guys can use it."

"No thanks," Adam said. "I mean, you did a nice job decorating this place and all, but it's still pretty creepy."

"Yeah," Jimmy agreed. "And it stinks pretty bad, too, doesn't it?"

"It sure does," Shauna and Jen said in unison.

"Don't worry, though," Jimmy assured them. "You'll get used to it."

"Why would we want to?" Dougie asked.

"Because creatures of the night need somewhere to go. I mean, you can't stay in your houses because your parents probably won't let you. The neighbors will talk and stuff. And you can't roam the streets because someone might catch you and take you to a laboratory, where they'll cut you apart and study your brain. So the only safe place you guys will really have to hide is down here."

Adam's blood started to chill.

"Why would we need to hide?" Chris asked nervously.

Just then, Itsy started to growl. But she wasn't growling at Jimmy, she was growling at Travis, who was standing beside them.

"What's the matter with you, you stupid mutt?" Travis growled back at Itsy.

"She's growling at your feet!" Eugene shrieked. "They're getting kind of funky!"

Adam blinked. Travis's sneakers had completely disintegrated. And his toes were twisting into two goatlike hooves!

"Does that answer your question?" Jimmy sneered at Chris.

"What's happening to me?" Travis cried out in a panic.

"You're stepping into my shoes now." Jimmy laughed.

Adam's head started to spin.

"So what time were you born?" Jimmy asked Travis.

"I don't know," Travis said. "A little after one A.M., I think."

"Well, that's what time it is now," Jimmy told him. "So you're transforming right on schedule. And lookey here," he mocked. "Your pal, Dougie, is starting to get pretty hairy, too."

173

Thick black hairs were shooting out of the pores on Dougie's face.

"Oh, man!" Dougie freaked. "I'm turning into a werewolf!"

"No." Jimmy laughed again. "You're turning into a beast."

Adam shot Jimmy a look, a red-hot fiery look.

"And I bet you were born at six after the hour," Jimmy told Adam. "Because that's what time it is now."

"You lied to me!" Adam growled as the top of his head started to throb.

"No, I didn't," Jimmy insisted. "I just didn't tell you the whole story. That's all."

"And what *is* the whole story?" Adam shouted.

Jimmy explained patiently. "In the witch club my mother belonged to, there was no curse-breaking, just curse-transference. That means you guys are now cursed. So every day at the hour of your births, you'll all turn into beasts. But don't worry," he told them. "Thirteen years after the moon is full on the thirteenth day of the months before your birthdays, you'll all know what to do to get out of it."

"What?!" Adam couldn't believe what he was hearing. "Are you kidding me with this?"

"Yeah." Jimmy laughed. "I'm just messing with you. The rules are different for curse-transference. You don't have to worry about the moon," he told Adam. "With curse-transference, the curse should only last thirteen months. Or maybe it's thirteen years. I forget. I'll have to ask my dad."

The throbbing in Adam's head began to split his skull as two horns started to grow.

"You can't do this to us!" Adam cried.

"I already have," Jimmy told them. Then he hocked a giant loogie and headed for the door.

"See you later, suckers!" His obnoxious voice echoed in the sewer pipe behind him.

Thanks to James Joseph Leeds, the beastly legend continued.

Don't miss the next spine-tingling book
in the DEADTIME STORIES® series

INVASION OF THE APPLEHEADS

Katie Lawrence was sure the torture would never end. She had to struggle to hold back the scream in her throat. Because she knew that if she screamed, things would only get worse.

That is, if things *could* get worse.

"Isn't this fun, kids?" Katie's mother asked cheerily.

No! Katie wanted to yell at the top of her lungs. *This is not fun! This is the worst possible way to spend a day!*

It was a beautiful, sunny Sunday. It was also the day before Halloween. That's what made things really bad.

Katie wanted to be home putting the finishing touches on her Halloween costume and getting ready for the big parade. The Halloween parade was the biggest event in Appleton. All of the kids in Katie's school were excited about it.

Katie was excited about it, too, especially since she'd been invited to a party by Christine Baker, the most popular girl in her class. Starting the fifth grade in a new school had been hard enough, but making new friends had been even harder.

Unfortunately, Katie wasn't at home right now working on her Halloween costume. Because Katie was crammed into the backseat of the car with her eleven-year-old brother, Andy, who didn't want to be driving around Appleton any more than she did. All because their parents had insisted they spend the day together visiting the town's historical sights.

"Are we going to stop soon?" Andy moaned.

"Yes," Mrs. Lawrence answered. "We're almost there."

"Almost where?" Katie whispered to her brother. "What stupid thing are we going to have to look at next?"

"Probably the biggest rock in Appleton," Andy whispered back.

They both snickered.

Katie and her family had moved to Appleton just a few months before. They used to live in the city, but Katie's parents had decided that a small town would be a much better place for them to grow up.

Appleton *was* a small town. It was a small *creepy* town, in Katie's opinion. It had been founded in the 1600s, and most of it still looked four hundred years old. Even the neighborhood Katie and her family lived in looked like a page from a history book.

Traveling through Appleton was like driving through a time warp. Except for the mall, there was nothing modern-looking at all.

Katie hated it.

But her parents adored it. They thought Appleton was the greatest place in the universe.

The morning before, Katie's mother had picked up a little guidebook at the library that told about all the historical sights in their new town. Before the day was over, they were going to visit every single one of them.

"I can't believe we spent twenty minutes looking

at a stupid piece of cement," Katie complained to Andy.

Even though Katie had whispered, her mother heard her. "What piece of cement?" she asked.

"The one that said 'George Washington crossed here,'" Katie answered. "What was so interesting about that?"

"That was very interesting," Mr. Lawrence answered. "It was the route that Washington took on his way to an important battle of the Revolution," he started to explain. "He—"

"I know. I know." Katie stopped her father. She couldn't stand to hear the story again. History was just about her least favorite subject in the world.

"So what are we going to see next?" Andy asked, sounding as impatient as Katie felt.

"The next stop is the Appleton Orchard," Mrs. Lawrence said, checking the guidebook.

Katie and Andy rolled their eyes.

"Do you want to hear what the guidebook says about it?" their mother asked.

"Nooooooo!" Katie and Andy answered at the same time.

"Of course we do," Mr. Lawrence said, shooting Katie and Andy a scolding look over his shoulder.

"I think you kids are really going to like this," their mother told them.

She'd been promising that all day. It hadn't been true yet.

"'The Appleton Orchard was originally owned by a woman who was accused of being a witch,'" Mrs. Lawrence read.

"Sounds pretty spooky, kids," Mr. Lawrence chimed in, trying to stir up their interest.

"Listen to this." Their mother continued to read. "'The townspeople believed that the witch was putting some kind of magic potion into her apples, a potion that turned all the children of Appleton into zombies. On Halloween Night, three hundred years ago, the angry parents burned the orchard to the ground.'"

"Pretty cool!" Andy said.

Katie agreed the story was cool, but she still wasn't

sure about going there. "If the orchard was burned to the ground, what is there to see?" she pointed out.

"The book says that the witch's house is still standing," her mother told her. "It's the oldest house in Appleton. And it wasn't even damaged in the fire."

Who wanted to see another stupid old house? Katie slumped against the car door. Things *had* gotten worse.

"Look at that," Mr. Lawrence said a second later as the orchard came into view.

A banner stretched across the road. It read WELCOME TO APPLETON ORCHARD.

There were hand-painted signs posted every few feet. *Free Candy Apples! Free Apple Cider! Free Haunted Hayrides!*

"I thought this place was supposed to be deserted," Katie said.

"Well, it certainly looks full of life today," her father replied as he drove toward the huge iron gates that led into the orchard. "Maybe someone has taken over the place. This looks like some kind of grand-opening celebration."

"That's funny," Mrs. Lawrence chimed in. "I didn't

see anything about it in the paper this morning. If I had, we could have skipped the sightseeing tour and spent the day here."

Katie shot her brother a look. Too bad there hadn't been anything in the paper. The orchard sounded a *little* more interesting than anything else they'd seen so far. Maybe they could have been spared a whole day of torture.

"Well, we're here now," Mr. Lawrence said, turning through the gates. "And we've still got a couple of good hours before it gets dark."

As they entered the grounds, Katie felt something strange. Something that made her shiver. It was as if she'd passed through some kind of invisible wall, or like diving into a pool and breaking through the surface of the water. And it happened just as quickly.

Strangely, outside the gates, the trees were turning colors and losing their leaves, but inside the gates, the apple trees were at their prime—green and loaded with fruit.

Katie turned around in her seat to look back at the gates.

Something else was wrong. But it took Katie a minute to figure out what it was.

Outside the gates, where the leaves on the trees were dying, it was a beautiful, sunny day. But inside the gates, where everything flourished, it was dark and dreary.

Katie shivered again. "Creepy," she said, talking to herself.

"What's creepy?" her mother asked.

"The trees," Katie answered. "How come they've still got apples?"

"Maybe the apple season is longer out here in the country," her mother said.

"But look how dark it is in here," Katie pointed out.

Her father laughed. "Of course it's dark," he said. "We're in the shadow of all these trees."

Katie caught a glimpse of the sky above the trees. It was steely gray, with no sunshine at all.

But before Katie could point that out to her family, the words stuck in her throat as a hideous creature stepped out from between the apple trees that lined the drive. Its head was swollen, and the green, putrid skin that covered its face was rotting right off its skull.

Bloodshot eyeballs hung from their sockets. And a blood-covered ax stuck out of its chest.

"Look!" Mrs. Lawrence exclaimed as another grotesque creature appeared ahead of them. "Everyone is dressed up for Halloween!"

Katie took a good look at the creature with the ax in its chest. If that was a costume, it was very, very good.

"This is excellent!" Andy said. "I definitely want to go on the haunted hayride."

"Didn't I tell you this would be fun?" Mrs. Lawrence said.

They pulled into the parking lot under a giant old shade tree where several other cars were already parked. But there were no other people in the parking lot, just the biggest, creepiest-looking scarecrow on a pole that Katie had ever seen.

Its head was the size of a basketball, and it was covered with a dirty white sheet that was tied around its neck with a thick, heavy rope dangling to the ground like a leash. Its face was painted onto the sheet.

The second her father parked the car, the creature started to move!

Katie let out a loud, startled cry.

So did her mother.

"It's all right," Katie's father assured them. "It's just someone dressed up in a Halloween costume."

The giant creature climbed down from its pole and started clomping its way toward them, flailing its arms and moaning. It looked like Frankenstein's monster dressed up as a scarecrow.

No one made a move to get out of the car.

"If he's trying to scare us away, he's doing a pretty good job," Katie's mother said nervously.

The scarecrow fell onto the hood of the car, moaning and groaning even louder than before.

"Let's get out of here!" Katie cried.

But it was too late.

Within seconds, the car was surrounded by cackling witches and blood-covered ghouls.

And Katie had the horrible feeling that they weren't just people in Halloween costumes.

ABOUT THE AUTHORS

As sisters, Annette and Gina Cascone share the same last name. As writers, they sometimes share the same brain. As children, they found it difficult to share anything at all.

The Cascone sisters grew up in Lawrenceville, New Jersey. It was there that Annette and Gina began making up stories. Since their father was a criminal attorney, and their mother claimed to have ESP, the Cascone sisters honed their storytelling skills early on in life—mainly to stay out of trouble. These days, they're telling their crazy stories to anyone who will listen.

Here are the stats: Gina is older; Annette is not. Gina

is married; Annette should be. Gina has two children; Annette borrowed one. Gina has a granddaughter; Annette has a grandniece. Gina has cats; Annette has dogs. They both have a sister named Elise.

Visit Annette and Gina at www.agcascone.com.

DEADTIME STORIES

Grave Secrets and *The Witching Game* movies star Disney's *Wizards of Waverly Place* JENNIFER STONE as the Babysitter.

Watch for all the *Deadtime Stories for Kids* films at:
www.DeadtimeStoriesTheMovie.com

Like us on Facebook and stay updated
on the books and movies, cast,
and exclusive behind-the-scenes information.

**Facebook: Deadtime Stories for Kids
and** The Beast of Baskerville